The Masters Review

ten stories

The Masters Review

The Masters Review Volume VIII
Stories Selected by Kate Bernheimer
Edited by Cole Meyer and Melissa Hinshaw

Front cover:
Design by Chelsea Wales

Interior design by Kim Winternheimer

First printing.

ISBN: 978-0-9853407-7-3

Printed in the USA

To receive new fiction, contest deadlines,
and other curated content right to your inbox,
send an email to newsletter@mastersreview.com

The Masters Review

ten stories

Volume VIII

Naïma Msechu • Lavanya Vasudevan

• Kate Bucca • Belal Rafiq •

Dawna Kemper • V. Efua Prince

• Lydia Martín • Jenna Geisinger •

H. de C. • Divya Sood

Stories Selected by Kate Bernheimer
Edited by Cole Meyer and Melissa Hinshaw

Contents

Editor's Note

In my junior year at the University of Wisconsin, I asked my creative writing professor for some advice. Workshops were helping me improve, yes, but I wanted to do more outside of the classroom. He suggested that I take up a readership with some literary journal, see the kinds of work that people are submitting for publication. I could see firsthand, then, what makes fiction (and creative nonfiction) truly work. We'd been spending the semester studying the craft masters—Alice Munro, George Saunders, Mary Gaitskill, Jhumpa Lahiri. It's something else entirely to read the unpublished work of an emerging writer and analyze on both a macro- and micro-scale whether a piece is successful. He suggested it would help me identify more readily the flaws in my own work, and that exposure to the slush pile would show me the kinds of stories editors are tired of seeing, because they're submitted over and again. He also said I would probably burn out in a year or so, but that the experience would be worth it.

He was right on two counts: My work with *The Masters Review* has undoubtedly made me a better writer, and a better reader. I know the kinds of stories I don't want to write, now, because I've read them so often, and in so many varieties. But he was wrong, too. It didn't burn me out. I'm coming up on my fifth year with *The Masters Review*, with hopefully many more ahead. I've served as a reader on all tiers, as an assistant editor to Sadye, and have now completed my first year as *The Masters Review*'s managing editor. It has been an absolute joy for me to see the progress of a submission in our queue, from newly submitted, to accepted and edited and finally published. In the editor's note for our sixth anthology, Sadye said that she felt like she had the easiest job in the world. That's a sentiment I can now safely echo. And I'll go one further: I get to read and edit the work of writers with such promising futures. I have the best job in the world.

Our mission has always been to provide a platform to emerging writers, writers who have a promising future ahead of them, writers who maybe just need that next publication to land an agent, or a book deal. And the anthology is at the heart of that: a collection of 10 fantastic writers at various points in their lives, in the world, in the stages of their writing career. In this anthology, we have writers who have won awards, who have been published only a handful of times, writers who have novels or collections out from small presses. What does it mean to be an emerging writer? In our last anthology, guest judge Rebecca Makkai said that when she was "emerging," for all she knew, it was a fluke. A mistake. But let me tell you: It's no mistake that these ten authors are collected here. They have all the promise in the world. Let them tell you their story.

—*Cole Meyer*
Managing Editor

Introduction

The Masters Review is a publication that relishes the fine art of writing in which we encounter form, technique, and story handled with dexterity, handled with grace. I appreciated all of the manuscripts sent to me for consideration by *The Masters Review* because I trust the editors to be very fine readers of craft. We know we are in the company of excellent readers when we pick up a copy of *The Masters Review*. Its editors and editorial staff work painstakingly to find beautifully and bravely written work whose authors respect the tradition and future of that mysterious technology still known to us as "writing." So I knew I could read the wonderful packet of manuscripts sent to me to consider for this special volume not as a writer scrutinizing technique, but as I prefer to read stories: simply to read them.

I don't drive like an engineer, eat cake like a baker, or go to the Egypt Room at the Met like a sarcographer. And most of the time, I read like a reader. When I am on the city bus, in a hospital waiting room, or at a diner, I read. I pass the time in company with someone I never have met, who has considered questions and situations I like to consider or never have considered. I read to enter humanity's big questions, to marvel at somebody else's way of understanding the world, to feel less alone. Even (gasp!)

to be entertained. Who was it who said there is no such thing as guilty pleasure reading, there is only *reading*? It may have been me who said this, in a class recently, but I'm uncertain of this! In any case, I agree.

Of course, as a practitioner of an art form—storytelling—I read widely and often. I appreciate well-timed paragraph breaks, parallel sentence structure, and surprising word choices. I adore how duration and interiority can operate so variously depending on who's done the writing that's printed in font inside of the book that I hold. But that's not how I read when I read as a reader. I *read to read*. I read for inspiration as a reader most of all, not for inspiration as a writer. I am a reader first. I read out of curiosity about my fellow human, who has imagined a difficult or beautiful or beautifully difficult world. I read to know what is possible, impossible, true.

And so the ten stories in this volume have been selected for publication because I loved reading them. They kept me good company. I think you will love reading them too. These are stories about people engaged in struggles and triumphs that are in turn surprising and familiar, in turn sad and sweet, in turn funny and grave. A lot of emotions you have had or wondered about, you will find in these pages. I was really impressed by the whole packet of stories sent to me by *The Master Review*, and there wasn't a story in the entire packet that I didn't read and feel something about as I read. These are the stories that drew me most to re-read them, and this is why they appear in the book.

Because when you read, you begin at the title, I want to list in alphabetical order each title that caught my attention immediately, and made me want to read the story's first sentence, and then the next, and the next, and the next . . . these are the words that began my journey as a reader through these stories. Relish this series: "American Crusader," "An English Woman and an Arab Man Walk into a Bar," "Chlorine," "Electric Guests," "Face to Face," "Fear," "June," "Lida," "Paper Boats," "Quiet Guest." These words, in the words of one of their authors, "release their heedless fragrance into the perilous air." Perilous air! The air of a story, the air that we breathe.

Congratulations to the writers, and welcome, readers.

—*Kate Bernheimer*
Guest Judge

Electric Guests

Naïma Msechu

Our vacation wasn't even halfway over when my brother ran into the living room, dropped the towel wrapped around his waist, and announced he had malaria. Our dad laughed.

"Malaria? I don't think so, Piper." He looked down at the crossword in his lap. "Go ask your mother."

"But look!" Piper said, walking closer to the couch our dad and I sat on. He pointed at his midriff. A speckled band of bug bites was strung from one hip bone to the other, standing out against the pale skin of his stomach like a string of bright red Christmas lights. His neck and upper arms, too, were ringed with clusters of them, and there were a few errant ones on his scrawny chest and upper thighs.

I snapped my book shut. "They're just bug bites."

He shook his head. "I think I got bitten by some kind of sea mosquito—a whole swarm of them. They got under my t-shirt and speedo when I was in the water this morning. I bet it's some weird foreign species."

"There's no such thing as sea mosquitoes," I said, though I wasn't completely sure. My brother was an enthusiastic hypochondriac (in the three weeks we'd spent at our beach house so far, he'd already falsely identified a melanoma and supposedly caught a foot fungus he was sure was deadly but no one else could see), and it was usually best to shut down his argument early. "No matter what you got bitten by, having tons of bug bites doesn't mean you have malaria."

"It's not just that," Piper said, scratching his neck. "I mean they started itching really bad as soon as I got out of the water and got worse when I was in the shower just now, but I also have a headache and a fever and my stomach feels weird." His voice sped up and rose in pitch as he talked, so that by the end his words sounded like the complaints of a very high-strung seagull.

I groaned. "Dad, does this seem likely to you?"

"Hold on, honey. Help me out real fast. What's it called when something's related to the supernatural? Has two c's in it."

I thought for a second. "No idea. Listen, Dad, he really thinks he has malaria."

"WebMD says so—my symptoms match the first stages."

"Highly unlikely." Dad tapped his pen on the newspaper. "It has a *t* in it, too."

"Come here, Piper," I sighed. My brother sat down on the couch and leaned his head toward me. I pressed my palm to his forehead with a little more force than necessary. It felt as warm as a towel left in the sun too long, but was nowhere near what I imagined to be a critically ill level. "I think you're just a little sunburnt."

"But my headache—and the nausea." He writhed on the couch, sending a few flecks of water flying from his head. "I think I need to go to the clinic. I feel very perilous."

Piper used words from our father's crosswords sometimes, with varying degrees of success. Dad was always shouting them out and they stuck to him like burrs from the brambles between our house and the beach, until he plucked them off and tested them in his mouth. *Sesquipedalian*, he'd mumbled, apropos of nothing, when I'd woken him up from a nap the day before. Last week, through a mouthful of breakfast cereal, *hygrometer*. I found them stuck in my mind too sometimes (this morning it had been *clairvoyant*), but usually I ignored them.

"I seriously doubt you need to go to the clinic. And dry off your hair. You're getting the couch all wet." I pointed to where the salmon-colored towel lay in a heap in the doorway like a discarded catch.

He shook his hair in my direction. "Dad, can I go to the clinic?"

"Because you think you have malaria? Piper, come on."

"I'm itchy and nauseous and I have a headache!"

Our dad laughed again. "Tara, this kid's sick in the head. He needs to be taken to the clinic."

"Seriously?" I glared at my brother.

"Why not," Dad said. He pointed his pen at Piper. "But son, put some clothes on. This is a civilized place, not a nudist colony."

Piper smirked at me and left the room, purposefully forgetting the towel on the floor. I dropped my book on the coffee table and paused in the doorway, ignoring the beached towel on principle. "When do we need to be back by?" I asked our dad, less because I cared and more because I wanted to tear him away from his crossword one last time.

"By dinner," he said. "We're having an early one. Let's say, in two and a half hours." I had almost reached the front door when I heard him yell, "Got it. *Occult*."

* * *

The diagnosis turned out to be better than Piper could ever have hoped for.

"Sea bather's eruption," the physician said sagely. "You were stung by jellyfish larvae."

Piper listened, eyes wide, as she explained. This was his favorite part of every medical issue, and at eight he was not yet old enough to know to disguise his excitement. What he had mistaken for sea mosquitoes were actually the early stages of thimble jellyfish, a species that could grow to the size of its namesake, but whose larvae were small as peppercorns. Piper had been lightly seasoned with jellyfish babies, I joked, but the physician only pursed her lips and my brother was too entranced to react. The t-shirt he had worn to ward off skin cancer and the skintight speedo briefs he thought protected him from other water-transmitted diseases had trapped the larvae against his skin. And so the fetal jellyfish, who were young but still developed enough to sting, had responded to this threat in the only way they knew how, leaving fiery scarlet bumps on his milky skin. Piper's shower, it seemed, had only made things worse.

"The larvae's nematocysts—those are their stinging cells—react to all sorts of changes," the physician said. "You would have been better off staying in the ocean, provided you found a spot free of all the larvae." Piper looked crestfallen, and his brows furrowed further when she added, "You have to be careful, because the nematocysts can sting even after the larvae die. I guess you could say they like to stick around and be a little mean."

Piper didn't fault the jellyfish for their stings. While I drove us back to our beach house, the late-afternoon sun beating down on our heads through the BMW's cracked-open convertible roof because he was afraid he hadn't gotten enough Vitamin D that day, all he could talk about was how sorry he felt for the jellyfish babies, how much he regretted kidnapping them from the water and leaving them to die.

"Is it futile? Do you think I could still save them?" he asked me. "Like maybe if I threw my shirt and shorts back in the water, some of them could still swim away?"

"I don't think so," I said quietly. I was proud of his correct use of the crossword burr, but more so surprised by how sad I felt. When I put Piper's clothes, towel, and swimwear into the washing machine before dinner, I realized that it wasn't that I cared about the jellyfish themselves. I wasn't even sure they had the power to think at that stage, if jellyfish thought at all. Probably, I hoped, they had barely felt their death. But even then, there was something tragic about creatures that stung after they had died, as if their ghosts couldn't help but stay behind to mourn their death and erect their own inflamed tombstones.

* * *

The news that my brother actually had a treatable condition barely garnered a response from our parents. It wasn't the first time he'd been right (though it didn't happen often), but even if it had been it wouldn't have mattered. Our parents couldn't be bothered either way, about Piper's hypochondria or much of anything else.

I couldn't pinpoint when it had started, only that it had intensified once I turned sixteen the previous April and could drive Piper around. They had fallen away even more when the summer started and we all spent more time at home. This vacation had only made it worse, but it had been a mistake no one could avoid, inevitable as the local ferry's hourly departures. We were a family, so we had to vacation in Florida.

The whole thing reminded me a lot of waiting for the ferry, too—not an anticipatory waiting, but the bored kind you do when you know the ferry will come on time because it always does, and you almost wish it would break the routine, but ultimately not because that would be inconvenient. In the past few weeks I had come to the realization that nothing in our family was wrong just as nothing was right. Worse, our parents' stubborn refusal to do anything about it made me feel like I'd uncovered a secret I wasn't supposed to, a truth that should have stayed hidden (and was hidden from Piper, as far as I knew) until I aged out of the family and couldn't be there to protest.

It was for this reason that I told our parents about the diagnosis and asked our mom to pass the salad in the same breath. Piper spent most of dinner dramatizing his run-in with the swarm of jellyfish larvae, all thoughts of malaria-carrying sea mosquitoes washed away.

"It's just too bad they're all dead," he concluded after twenty minutes, looking around for approval.

"Mmm, that *is* sad," Mom said, looking past him toward the clock on the opposite wall. She had a yoga class she needed to get to soon, as she'd already reminded us several times.

"Damn shame," our dad said, looking into his lap at the crossword we all knew was there. "Better luck next time, son."

*   *   *

That night, Piper broke out in chills. I'd already helped him smear hydrocortisone cream on the stings after dinner, but around 11 p.m. he tiptoed into my room and complained he was cold.

I put down my book about reincarnated love in ancient Egypt and felt his forehead. "You're burning up."

Piper crept into my bed. "I don't feel hot, though. I feel cold and my head hurts and I feel a little sick." He pulled the covers right up to the scar on his chin that he'd gotten from crashing his tricycle when he was three. His hands were shaking slightly.

"A little sick how?" I gave him an exaggerated side-eye. "You're not gonna puke on me, are you?"

Piper, normally not immune to well-timed potty humor despite his sophisticated medical knowledge, merely shook his head. "I just feel weird. Still itchy, and kind of tingly. Kind of like I've been electrocuted."

I thought for a second. It had happened before, when he was five. He'd stuck a fork in our toaster at home in New York and had been lucky to only get a moderate shock. If he had done something like that recently, though, he would have told me about it right away. Now, my mind pictured tiny jellyfish ghosts hovering around the inflamed graveyard beneath the thin cotton of my brother's pajamas before I could stop it. As much as my brother annoyed me sometimes, I didn't think he deserved a midsummer haunting. "The physician prescribed you some steroid pills in case you felt worse. Wanna try those out?"

He nodded, eyes closed.

When I returned to the room with the bottle of prednisone pills, my bed was empty. The word *haunting* came back into my mind, unbidden, like one of our dad's crossword burrs though not from any crossword I could remember, then my stomach felt like it did when I tried to swing, like rising and falling all at once.

Crossword burrs didn't feel like much of anything when discovered. This was something different.

I heard retching from the bathroom down the hall and found Piper sitting on the floor in front of the toilet bowl. "I thought you said you weren't gonna puke?" I asked, sitting down beside him. He didn't answer, only stared at the murky water in the toilet bowl. "Ding-dong." I pulled on his earlobe like I had done all the time when he was younger. "Anybody home?"

He began humming. It was a low sound, barely slipping through his closed lips like an eel through an underwater crevice. The charged melody wound itself around the toilet bowl, around me, around him. I knew without knowing how that he was wrapping himself in something quietly electric, and mournful, a sadness both his and not his. And with the same rising and falling feeling as before came the word *dirge*.

The label shocked me into opening my mouth. "Piper, stop." He didn't. I noticed the bottle still in my left hand and took out a pill. "Piper, look at me." He didn't, so I squeezed myself between him and the toilet and forced the pill between his lips. "Swallow," I ordered, and he did, the humming breaking off for one long moment before picking back up. "Piper, you can stop now."

But he did not stop for over an hour. I sat with him for a while, holding his flushed hands with my back pressed against the cool toilet bowl. Eventually I couldn't stand the swinging feeling in my stomach anymore and left him there on the turquoise tiles, rocking slightly and humming, cocooning himself in a song that seemed unable to reduce the chills generated by the phantom electricity buzzing in his veins.

*　*　*

Piper was different after that. He became less nervous and his medical anxiety all but disappeared. It was almost like my brother had been replaced by a doppelgänger (one of Dad's new favorite words; it had been the final one in his most recent crossword, which he had completed while I was telling our parents about Piper's night in the bathroom, to which he had replied, "He hummed? The boy needs to use his words, build a vocabulary," and handed Piper the completed puzzle). I was the only one in the family who spent enough time with him to notice the eerie change and realize that the jellyfish larvae had never truly left him.

He called them his electric guests. They made his entire body shiver perpetually, as though he couldn't quite feel comfortable on land and had to create his own waves in the air particles around him to navigate through them. His movements were an endless cycle of small advances and retreats, like the expanding and contracting of the jellyfish whose ghosts clung to his body. They slowed him down, but he seemed unbothered. He continued to read—though his books were now about the ocean instead of about diseases—and spent hours on his Nintendo, even as the restlessness remained.

I found I couldn't stay in a room with him for long, and began to establish hiding places where I hoped he wouldn't find me, and still he did. Still he found me, entering the room quietly, purposeful and hesitant at the same time, his body surging and receding infinitesimally, all while walking toward me on feet so quiet I could never hear him coming, feet that were always moist and actively leaked when he got excited, betraying his movements with the shallow curved puddles they left behind on the hardwood floors. I always wiped them up before our parents noticed (an unlikely event in and of itself), keeping the secret for both of us. My fear was that, if our parents realized something was wrong, they would send him away for treatment and leave me to spend the last few weeks with them, alone. The leaking seemed to mean that water was a large part of what sustained him, and I worried about what it meant that he was leaving so much of it behind. I knew that any doctor I took him to would notify our parents, so I began to force him to medicate by drinking a gallon of water a day, dreading the end of summer and our inevitable return to the parched concrete of the city.

"Tara," he would say when he found me sitting in a closet or behind an armchair. Even the way he talked had changed. He expelled the first half of the word and sucked the second half back into his mouth, as if my pebble of a name was too much effort and he needed to take it back to have the strength to say more.

I would smile at him, with teeth, and he would simply raise the corners of his mouth. Finding me wasn't a game to him, like it would have been a few weeks ago. Poking his pale arm only elicited a small "hey," no trace of indignation or coming revenge. He had come on a mission.

"Go to the beach with me."

And I did, since it was the only place I could stand to be near him. We went to our house's quiet portion of the beach every day, and he spent hours wading through chest-high water, naked now to deter new guests. I stayed on the shore and kept reading my way through the serial Egyptian love story, glancing up from my historical fiction occasionally to make sure he wasn't getting too far away as he explored his historical reality.

Because that was what it was: Piper seemed older, seemed to carry the history of the ocean, memories of thousands and thousands of years of oceanic happenings corralled by his permanently splayed fingers, which were never still except when he was in the water. There, his limbs slowed, gliding through the water as if they were part of it. He told me things about the ocean every chance he got, tales of fabled dangers in the travelling seaweed forests and descriptions of the way this stretch of beach had looked long ago. When I asked, he told me he'd learned the information from the books he read, but sometimes I caught him whispering to the ocean, his lips gliding just above its surface before darting below to catch the answer.

*   *   *

A week after the death of the electric guests, our family had fruit punch Jell-O for dessert. It was another Friday, the only day all of us had dinner together, and Mom served it after we'd finished the lasagna. She had bought it premade and put it into a large round serving bowl that had come with the house, which would have been endearing if the Jell-O's original packaging hadn't been square shaped. Jagged fissures gave away where she had struggled to transplant it.

"Dessert time!" she chimed.

"Yay," I said flatly.

"I thought Jell-O was your favorite?" she asked, handing me a bowl of it. I looked inside and saw she'd sliced it into slimy gelatinous chunks. When I stuck my spoon in the bowl, the red Jell-O jiggled like a slow-motion electrocution.

"It was, three years ago."

"Oh," she said. "And you, Piper?"

Piper was staring into his bowl with something between trepidation and excitement. It took me a second to guess that eating Jell-O was a way to honor his electric guests at best and symbolic cannibalism at worst. Our parents registered nothing.

"Hmm, Piper?" Dad asked. His crossword was out, lying beside his bowl as if he hoped the Jell-O would give him clues in its jerky Morse code. His word-finding was something of an addiction in the summer (he was the head of a bank and often said he didn't want to have anything to do with numbers while he was on vacation), and Mom allowed him to take the puzzle out during dessert.

My brother looked up, biting his lip. "Yeah, I like it okay." Our parents looked at him expectantly. He picked up his spoon—his shivering hands making the metal throw a shard of reflected light from the lamp overhead onto the table—and plunged it into the Jell-O. When the spoon resurfaced, it shook and the Jell-O shook with it.

"What do you have now, Parkinson's?" Dad teased. It was the first time either of our parents had acknowledged his shakiness.

My brother glanced at me and I nodded. There was no way around it. His mouth accepted the offering with its usual forward and backward movement, slurping the Jell-O off the spoon and pulling away a moment later. As soon as he tasted it, his eyes widened. He smiled.

"Do you like it?" Mom asked.

"M-hm," he said, his voice stronger than usual, the sound bisected more clearly.

She pushed her chair back from the table. "Good. I'm heading off to the studio to finish glazing a few pots. I've got to put in some extra hours if I want to be done in time for the next show, so I won't be back until late."

"Good luck, honey," our dad said, eyes on his crossword. As soon as she left the house, he excused himself and went to the back porch with his bowl. I was left in the kitchen with the buzzing overhead light, the quivering Jell-O, and my shaking brother.

"Isn't it weird for you, eating Jell-O?" I asked him.

Piper shook his head. "It's not made from jellyfish." He paused. "Is it?"

"No," I laughed. "But the consistency—"

"Is perfect. It's so easy to eat." He grinned, teeth extra white between stained lips, and I felt something wet on my foot. I yelped and looked under the table.

"Your feet are leaking again!" I said, not bothering to be quiet even though the door to the porch was open, because I knew Dad was too busy navigating his semantic ladder system to hear. *Meniscus.* The burr seemed to appear just to spite me and I batted it away in my mind.

"Sorry." Piper didn't look up from his bowl.

"Well you're gonna have to dry things up yourself," I said. "I'm going upstairs."

He looked like he was going to say something, then lifted the bowl to his face. His cheeks moved in a regular rhythm as he sucked out the Jell-O: balloon, collapse, repeat. I took my bowl to the kitchen and emptied it into the dishwasher, spreading the clumps out evenly among the plates our mom had rinsed before leaving the load for me to start. The Jell-O oozed down the sides of the white plates and bowls, slimed up shiny glasses, and collected on the sharp ridges of silverware and in puddles on the inside of the dishwasher door. I left the dishwasher open, knowing full well that the soppy crime scene would not phase whichever of our parents eventually saw it, that my brother might even close and start the dishwasher himself when he was done eating, and anyway that the evidence would inevitably be washed away. Tomorrow we would eat on the same plates again, and no one but me would feel the fruit punch in our food.

*   *   *

Once and only once I took Piper to the aquarium. Most of our days began with a slow, sleepy morning followed by an afternoon beach visit, varied only by a trip to the local library when we needed to stock up on more books. That morning a coupon had been left in our mailbox and I'd decided it was an omen, even though the reduced price didn't matter. Before she went to her studio or yoga class, Mom always left her credit card on the kitchen table in the decorative bowl she'd made herself, saying we could use it "within reason" and to just not "get carried away." She was always saying things like that, warnings that sounded like she'd read them in a magazine about parenting but that lacked any kind of conviction. I'd learned long ago that her reprimands were like the salmon she served when she was feeling ambitious: missing the tiny sharp bones you had to watch out for with other fish. Dad was different. He was rarely home during the year and when he was around in the summer he was determinedly solitary, yet when he deviated from his joking tone, we listened. The only thing he said when our mom first left the credit card for us was, "Don't buy drugs."

I grabbed the card and ushered Piper toward the driveway. It glinted as I shoved it into my pocket. I'd never had the guts to test it, but I assumed it was bottomless.

The aquarium was in a brick building near the center of town. It was pitifully small compared to the one we'd visited in the city just that spring. Then, Piper had been bored, more fixated on the kinds of harmful mold that could be lurking in the water filters than the actual animals. The new Piper was, as it turned out, disgusted too, but for a different reason.

"They're trapped," he said, his face inches from the glass of a wall-sized tank behind which brilliantly colored fish swam in aimless loops. "They can't get out."

"That's kinda the point of an aquarium, Piper," I said.

He turned to me accusingly. "They want to be in the ocean."

"Let's go look at the crabs," I said, noticing the water beginning to seep out of the holes in the sides of the Crocs I'd made him wear, onto the already wet linoleum. It seemed no creature here could contain its leaking.

"Do you think they keep families together?" he asked when we reached the touch tank, in which sea urchins, horseshoe crabs, and stingrays idled.

"What?"

"When they bring them here from the ocean. Do you think they split up families?"

I dipped a finger into the water, then recoiled when a stingray swam toward it. "I don't know. I think it'd be pretty hard to tell what a family looks like."

Piper withdrew his hand from the pool. "I bet they don't keep them together."

He was silent for the rest of the exhibits, and when we reached the jellyfish one he demanded to leave without even looking at it. He pushed through the glass-paneled door so hard he made the wooden fish that hung on a string inside it clatter and swing wildly. There was nothing for me to do except follow him into the parking lot. WE HOPE TO SEA YOU AGAIN SOON a sign at one edge of the driveway said, and Piper aimed a mouthful of spit at it as we drove away.

*   *   *

Time sped up as the end of the summer neared, the month of August folding in on itself like a deflating pool mattress. Piper seemed to nourish himself solely from water, Jell-O, and facts about the ocean. He accompanied me on my weekly shopping trips, trailing behind me while I picked up the essentials. He wore his Crocs and knew to keep his shaking and halting movements to a minimum, but in the end it was not something he could control. I developed a habit of using my body to shield him from the view of other shoppers, my eyebrows always fractions away from a glare. Whether it was this ready hostility or an instinctive suspicion on the part of the shoppers that there was something wrong with my jellyfish brother, we ended up alone in every aisle not long after we'd entered it.

"Don't worry," Piper would say when he noticed my eyebrows had in fact dropped to their lowest position. "Everyone wishes they had electric guests—those people are just jelly." And I would laugh in spite of myself at his lame pun.

When we entered the Jell-O aisle at the end of the shopping trip, it was his turn to smile. I let him pick out seven boxes to tide him through the week, and as soon as we got home they were transformed into a pyramidal shrine in his closet—berry blue and strawberry banana and island pineapple and lime stacked three, two, one, one, a rainbow pyramid with a black cherry tip, always a black cherry tip because that was his favorite.

After dinner, when our mom had gone off to her studio and our dad was on the back porch with his crossword, we made Jell-O and carried it in brimming bowls to the beach. Piper always wanted to sit as close to the receding water as possible, watching it while he ate from his bowl, and I read with a flashlight and sat close enough so I could keep an eye on him, but far enough so that the sound of the waves drowned out his slurping sounds. We'd spend at least an hour there, on sand the ocean had forgotten about for the night. Sometimes we would find other abandoned creatures—horseshoe crabs and mussels and, occasionally, a jellyfish or two.

Then Piper approached the gelatinous carcass and drew a shaky circle around its motionless form. "So the ocean knows where to find him tomorrow morning," he said. He hummed as he worked and I recognized the tune as the dirge. But as soon as he had memorialized all the jellyfish bodies, he would stop humming, and when I asked him to repeat it later, he said he had already forgotten how the tune went.

*   *   *

On the night before our last day of vacation, Piper called the electric guests his family.

My head was in the fridge, checking on the Jell-O we wanted to take with us to the beach. When I turned to him, he held out the book he was reading, which was opened to a taxonomic tree of jellyfish in the Coronatae order. "Look," he said again. "It's my family."

"*Their* family, you mean," I corrected automatically, closing the fridge and sitting down on the stool next to him at the kitchen island.

"No, mine."

"No." I nudged him. "I'm your family. Mom is your family. Dad is your family."

Piper didn't answer. I watched his index finger move down the page, tracing the lines until he reached the thimble jellyfish. *Coronatae, Linuchidae, Linuche.* "*Linuche unguiculata*," he whispered, and then, more loudly, "I think the ocean wants to keep me. I think that's why it sent me the electric guests."

"Well, the ocean can't have you." I ripped the book from his hands and slid it across the island so hard it fell onto the floor. Piper winced but stayed seated. It was the first time I'd yelled at him since the arrival of the electric guests. "Tell the jellyfish that," I continued. "They can't have you. Their family is big enough."

Next thing I knew, I was angry, angrier than I'd been in a long time. My face was starfish pink in the reflection of the microwave when I stood up.

I took the bowl from the fridge and turned to Piper. "Grab your towel and all your boxes of Jell-O. We're going to the beach."

"But it's not—"

"Just do it," I said quietly, and for some reason he complied.

The beach was just like it was any other night, but in my rage everything seemed sharper. The nearly full moon glinted and illuminated the sand, and even then I managed to overlook and step on the jagged edge of a broken shell.

I cursed and shook my beach bag off my shoulder. "We're stopping here." Piper hadn't spoken since we left the house, but from how fast his shadow vibrated on the sand I could tell he was worked up.

"What—" he started.

"Drop your towel, bring your Jell-O boxes."

"But Tara—"

"The Jell-O boxes."

His brow was furrowed with concern, but I didn't care if I was scaring him. I turned and walked toward the ocean. By the time he reached it, I had already dumped the bowl of premature Jell-O into the water.

"Tara!"

"Hand me a box."

"No!" He turned and ran, and I followed, dodging detritus. He was fast, but I was faster, and stronger. I tackled him just outside our house's portion of the beach, our heads falling inches from a beached jellyfish. I cursed again, but held onto Piper until he stopped struggling. Then he was crying, his face glistening like the jellyfish beside us. I pulled the box out of his hands and shook its contents into the water, the powder blossoming green while he sobbed into the sand a few feet away. His cries sounded eerily submarine, somewhere between boy and whale, something of the deep. I retrieved our things from further up the beach and spread out the towels on dry sand near the brambles that separated us from the houses. I noticed he was shaking.

"Come here, Piper."

He was crying more softly and had started humming the dirge. Still, he crawled onto the towels with me.

"Why'd you do that?" he asked when his breathing and shaking were as regular as the electric guests allowed.

I reached into my bag and pulled out a family photo album I'd found under one of Mom's pots in the TV cabinet on our way out of the house. I pointed my flashlight at it. "Look."

He began humming again and made a movement like he was about to get up. I wrapped both arms around him, half hug, half capture, until I was sure he wouldn't try anything. Then I showed him pictures of when we were little: him two and pudgy and me eleven and gangly, pushing him on a swing; him five on Christmas morning, Mom and Dad each holding one of his hands as he sat on his new bike; him on the first day of first grade, me starting tenth but posing in a matching t-shirt because he'd wanted to. I illuminated and recollected and exaggerated until he fell asleep, the humming petering off like an unfurling tentacle. I silently hoped it was the last time I'd ever hear it.

At some point Piper's arms had slid around my torso, and I had to pry his clasped fingers apart one by one before I could stand. He had managed to hide the box of black cherry Jell-O under a pile of sand, but after I accidentally stepped on it, I saw the last two, berry blue and island pineapple, lying exposed nearby. I dumped them onto the sand a little way off, having decided seconds before that adding them to the water might be too symbolic of creation, of revival, and that it would be more destructive to leave them dry.

I was flying by the seat of my pants, like Mom liked to say about her pottery practice, but I had no other choice. In the middle of my earlier tackle I had seen a flash of another word, clear as a crossword line: *exorcism*. Now that the rising and falling feeling in my stomach had passed, I was operating under the simple logic of 5-Across, and it told me to stay on the beach with my brother.

In the morning, his shudders were shallower, and when he tried to hum, the melody sounded off even to me. He asked to go home, said he was thirsty, but I shook my head. I forced him to stay out there with me, a safe distance from the water, for four more hours, stay until the sun was high in the sky, stay even after he'd spotted the dark red remains of his beloved black cherry. Both of us had stripped, me to my underwear and Piper to his skin, and we lay side by side like some ridiculous parody of casual tanning. It was a Monday late in the season, so hardly anyone saw our glazed bodies or heard the stories I told him, stories of first bike ride, of crayon squiggles on kitchen wall, of first tooth lost a few years before. He stayed quiet, but I took that as a good sign, especially when I noticed his shudders softening further, like ice cream left in the sun.

At 2 p.m., he asked if he could get into the water, his voice so thin it was barely there. His body was still.

"No," I rasped, "but you can go back to the house."

*   *   *

I locked him in the house for the rest of the day while our parents packed for our evening departure, refusing to let him out even when they, filled with the euphoria of an almost-endured eight-week vacation, offered to go on a sunset walk along the beach with us. They went anyway, and I locked the door behind them, turning just in time to see Piper leave the kitchen.

He was waiting for me at the top of the stairs with a partially opened box of Jell-O, two of his sunburned fingers caked with yellow powder.

"Piper, what the—"

"It tastes different," he said, licking his fingers and dipping them back into the box.

I was taken off guard. "Well, duh. It's powder."

"No, but even in my mouth, when it's wet. It doesn't taste as good. It bothers my palate."

I held out my hand, ignoring the misused crossword burr. "I don't care where you stashed it, just give it to me. We're leaving in less than an hour."

Piper shrugged. "I don't want it anyway. It's pretty unhealthy." He handed the box to me and walked off toward his room. When I flicked on the hall light, I noticed his feet had left behind spots of moisture, bright and round like tiny moons, waning as I watched.

NAÏMA MSECHU received her B.A. in Literary Arts from Brown University in 2017. She now spends her time between Germany and the United States, both of which she calls home. Her writing has appeared in The Postscript Journal, Thin Noon, and Wigleaf, among others, and her stories have received honorable mentions from Glimmer Train Press.

American Crusader

Lavanya Vasudevan

I s there anything more American than being in the right place in the right time, and seizing the opportunity when it presents itself? Would Miller be where he is now, if he hadn't been right there on set as a volunteer crew member, rigging up the soundboard, right at the moment when Brett McCormack left in a huff because he'd wanted a bigger role, causing Scott, the director of the Second Stage, to notice this short brown dude tripping over himself to get out of Brett's way, and say, hey, didn't you audition with us last week?

True, the teacher of the Meisner Foundations class, which Miller attended four days a week for twelve weeks, did call Miller's scene one of the bravest and most truthful performances he had ever seen. At the American Dialect Studio which Miller attends every Sunday morning without fail, they call his progress amazing, his Indian accent practically nonexistent. He has even changed his name to *Miller*, which—though he did not realize is a surname, not a first name—will be far easier to spell and pronounce than *Balamuralikrishnan*. Still, when he lands the role of a traitor that the American Crusader kills by the end of the first act, no one is more surprised than Miller himself. At home by himself that

Saturday night, he celebrates by opening a bottle of the cheapest beer he can find.

By the second week of rehearsals, Miller can no longer wake up early enough to TA the Introduction to Machine Learning class which allows him to pay his share of the rent. When Miller calls home to tell his parents, ask them for a loan, his father's thin voice stretches across the miles, and winds itself around Miller's ears like a noose. He reminds Miller that they are paying for his fancy PhD in computer science, not so he can fritter away his time playing pretend like a child, but so that he can get a job, buy a house, find a wife, live a better life than they ever did. Miller's brother, however, laughs out loud when Miller tells him the plot of the play. It is about a timid, cautious astronomy professor called Archie Masters who endures a blast of atomic radiation, gains superhuman abilities, turns into the American Crusader, and saves the world from Nazis. Swaminathan tells Miller about their cousin, who is homeless and about to get deported, after ten years of working as an IT consultant, now that his visa has expired. Although Miller has fortified himself for the call with three pints, he hangs up without telling Swami his other news, that he has started dating a white girl who happens to be a full-time actor.

Miller likes being around Kiersten because she smells like jasmine, which, for Miller, brings up the fading memory of silver-haired women in red and gold saris sitting cross-legged at the market in scorching summer, patiently weaving the flowers into a garland for a bride-to-be. Miller works up the nerve to ask Kiersten about her perfume, and she shows him her travel spray bottle of Be You, which features notes of vanilla, amber, and musk, but no jasmine. The sticker on the back promises that the wearer will be amazingly sexy, while still being completely themselves, without even having to try. Miller is emboldened to text Kiersten and ask her out, and embarrassed to find out that he has misspelled her name. He can never remember how many *e*'s and how many *i*'s and in what order, especially after a six-pack, but Kiersten says it's no big deal. Miller resolves to make it up to her by having her over for dinner and cooking the meal himself.

What Miller cooks for dinner is lasagna, which he has learned to make by watching the *Great British Baking Show*. While watching the show, Miller is seized by sudden doubt—should he have spent all these months picking up a British accent instead? It does not blend in, but does it not stand out in the best possible way? If he had gone into auditions sounding British, he might have snared a bigger role—maybe even the Nazi who dies in the third act.

During dinner, Kiersten tells Miller that she was hoping he would make curry. She loves curry; in fact, she goes to this place in La Brea every week; maybe they could go together next time. Miller holds the fork with his left hand, the knife with his right, and imagines Kiersten eating sambar rice with her fingers. The idea seems so unnatural, so alien to him that it is almost repugnant. He takes a sip of his IPA and tells her he very rarely goes out to Indian restaurants; really, what would be the point? While Kiersten is in the bathroom, Miller goes over to the hall closet and finds her jacket. At first, it smells like stale cumin. Then a whiff of yeasty bulldog, and the earthy odor of Kiersten's perspiration. And underneath all these layers of fusty spice, dog funk, and sweat, Miller catches the faint, intoxicating bouquet of jasmine. He presses the jacket to his face and inhales the scent, breathing deeper and deeper until he feels his chest is about to burst.

In the lab, Miller's machine-learning system is no longer behaving as it should. Miller has spent four years training his neural network model with thousands of hours of speech recordings, tens of thousands of images. And yet, when asked to serve up a picture of *blue eyes,* it stubbornly returns brown; *blond hair* retrieves an uncompromising black. Is the software faulty—but surely, he can overhaul the software—or is it the hardware that has doomed him from the start? Miller's lab mate, Lee, whose parents are both alumni, puts an arm around Miller's shoulders and assures him that no one gives a damn. Lee opens the mini fridge he keeps under his desk, and hands Miller a bottle of something he says costs two hundred dollars and is banned in twelve states. "Twenty-eight percent ABV, man," he says. "Are you Buddhist? No? Doesn't matter. It's gonna open the portal to your higher self, man." Miller accepts the invitation to walk through the portal, but his higher self is not sitting cross-legged under a Bodhi tree, waiting to dispense the wisdom of the world. He seems to have gone away, abandoned Miller, without giving the smallest of damns.

In the uncertain light of the early morning, Miller walks back to his apartment outside of campus, past a gray-haired man standing at the bus stop. The man looks at Miller, and his face lights up, as if he has recognized an old friend. "Excuse me," he says in a familiar cadence, "Are you from India?" Miller cringes as though he has been caught in a crime. He nods, carefully, unwilling to commit himself further. The man switches to Hindi. "Son," he says, "can you tell me which bus I am to take to get to," he consults a piece of paper that trembles in his hands, "to Artesia?" Miller has been to Artesia. The man must take three buses to get there from downtown. That is when Miller realizes he has forgotten how to say *three* in Hindi. It is not his fault—it's not like Hindi's his native tongue anyway—it's been years—why did he pick Miller of all people—who does he think—why did he call him *son*? "*Perdon*," Miller blurts out, "no hablo español." Then he turns and flees, unable to look back at the man, unable to face the disappointment that must surely be writ large on his wrinkled face.

That afternoon, Miller finds out that his thesis advisor is furious that Miller is running lines from some play instead of the algorithms that will make or break his graduate thesis. The message "shape up or ship out" is conveyed to Miller, not by the professor himself, but by one of his inexhaustible army of postdoctoral fellows. Miller looks at Lee, who shrugs and mouths, *fuck him*. When Miller, in increasing desperation, confides in his brother, Swami responds in an almost pitch-perfect imitation of Miller's accent: "You do you, man." But Miller cannot explain why he finds it far easier to perform other characters than to do himself. He has tossed aside the script he came in with, and grasped at another, but the lines are blurring, the words are melting into nothingness, and he is left to slip and slide on a crowded stage, sweating under the lights, with no one to feed him the next line.

At the final dress rehearsal, Miller struggles to reproduce the bravery and truth that had once distinguished him in acting class, despite the portal-opening elixir that he has downed, quickly and furtively, before entering the theatre. When Miller asks Scott to remind him what his motivation is again, Scott asks Miller what the fuck is wrong with him. Kiersten wonders if it would help if they all just took five, and Miller weaves his way to the restroom. Miller pleads with the mirror, strives to summon up the compelling abs, the stern shoulders, the pitiless mouth of a villain worthy of opposing the Crusader himself. Instead, the mirror looks back at him with the downtrodden eyes of his disgraced cousin, and Miller finds this so unbearable that he throws up. Miller tells himself that it is not vomit that emerges from his mouth, but coil upon coil of jasmine. He imagines hundreds and thousands of round white, waxy flowers, each one swirling with whorls of starry petals that open and release their heedless fragrance into the perilous air.

Miller returns from the bathroom, goes up to the stage, and finds his mark. Kiersten turns to him, her face glowing under the harsh lights, her eyes inviting him to be anyone he wants to be. Miller ignores her and looks at Scott. His voice rings out in fine, bold American dialect. "Hey, man," he says, "Can we run it again from the top?"

The narrator reads out from the wings: "The American Crusader is capable of flight, superhuman strength, and invulnerability to bullets. The full extent of his powers at this time is unknown."

LAVANYA VASUDEVAN was born in a large city in South India that has since renamed itself. She is a recovering software engineer who lives near Seattle and reviews children's books for Kirkus. Her short fiction has appeared or is forthcoming in Jellyfish Review, Atticus Review, The Southeast Review, and elsewhere. Find her on the web at www.lavanyavasudevan. com and on Twitter @vanyala.

Chlorine

Kate Bucca

Dahlia spewed cuss words in regular conversation, back before we saw swears as common parts of speech. Back when our eleven-year-old breasts just started to push out against our tight Speedos and the brave girls among us stripped off their suits to shower. Back when we first began gauging ourselves against each other, clamoring both to love and cut down.

If Dahlia had acted nonchalant, even defiant, she'd have ruled us. Thrown in an intentional curse or two—*what the* hell *is Coach thinking?* or *Kelsie is such a* bitch!—and all the girls would have fallen down fawning, trying to keep up with her random blips. *So cool.* But once we discovered that she didn't mean to swear, that she wasn't beyond-her-years rebellious, that she actually had no control over herself, we jumped on the difference. Belonging required acts of exclusion to reinforce your own place in the group.

She told us about her disorder on her first day of swim practice as we stood at the end of the lanes waiting for our set of instructions, absentmindedly tugging at the Lycra bands sliding up our butts. Jessie never pulled down her suit, allowed the edges to ride high; turned her back to the boys hovering a lane over so they'd see. Dahlia stared at the high ceiling of our cavernous pool, the practice arena for a serious Midwestern sport. Rafters strung with flags in goldenrod and maroon, the Orland Orcas's signature colors. A wall of banners proclaiming the team's championship victories. The girls' team had a shot of taking back the title that year.

Dahlia held out her hand like an awkward salesman hawking goods at our door. *Friendship, for sale.* She tapped her teal silicone swim cap against her pudgy thigh. Yanked down the edges of her knock-off suit, cheap navy nylon with white American flags. We snickered at the suit, our own bodies clad in the season's new fabric—thin, slippery striped material made to mimic sharkskin— that contoured every ripple of rib, every extra deposit of fat. Not yet old enough for weigh-ins or coach-mandated diets, we'd recently begun a game of pinching our bodies with fingers like calipers, comparing our layers of *extra*. Jessie initiated the ritual, so she presided over the verdicts.

The new girl had been transferred to our team by overprotective parents after an undisclosed incident during an Antioch Albacores practice. A few days before Dahlia arrived, Coach had given us a pep talk about the importance of bonding and making our new teammate feel welcome. Why do adults persist in singling out a kid for inclusion, drawing more attention to someone who'd benefit most by blending in? We, of course, responded by speculating for months, often in front of our target, about exactly what humiliation Dahlia had suffered on the other team.

When Jessie refused to shake hands that first day, Dahlia slipped out *shit* and reddened from her forehead, covered with the wet wisped strands of hair from a prepractice rinse, to her back straining against the tight suit. We pounced, emboldened by the display of weakness.

"Control yourself," Jessie snickered.

"I can't help it," Dahlia whispered. "It's called Tourette syndrome."

Looking around our semicircle, Jessie calculated our commitment. Knew we awaited her judgment of the new girl.

Three years earlier, when we were a bunch of eight-year-olds sitting on the grooved aluminum on-deck bleachers for the first time, nervously eying our new teammates, the blond teenage boy with the biggest muscles walked by, trailed by a pack of friends, on the way to the locker rooms. He paused to assess us, leaning on the railing in front of our seats. Ogling us with a hunger we were only beginning to understand.

Singling out Jessie for her red hair—an easy difference—he taunted, "Fire crotch!" The boys around him sneered.

Jessie raised her chin. "Du-uhhhh." She looked around at each of us before raising one eyebrow and turning to the boy. "Not that *you'll* ever get to see."

We'd been clamoring after her ever since.

Staring at Dahlia, Jessie shook her fiery curls, *tsk*ing in mock disappointment. "Can't help it? So, you're just naturally a disgusting pig? Potty-mouth piggy."

We laughed, some of us shifting around nervous weight. All of us searching for another insult to impress Jessie.

"Potty-mouth piggy. PMP, sounds like pimp. We've got a pimp on our hands, girls," attempted Amanda, side-glancing around the circle. At eleven, we were growing aware of sex-as-power and the illicit nature of any comment referencing it. Amanda's older brother let her watch R-rated movies, sitting close to him on the couch, when her parents weren't home. She provided a source for descriptions of the seedier parts of the sexual world. A few of us snickered at her comment, not wanting to seem like we didn't understand, but when no one repeated the insult, she reclaimed favor with "potty-mouth piggy!"

Fuck, beep, beeeeep, shit. Dahlia clenched her fists and moved to leave the circle.

"Why are you beeping, piggy?" Jessie shoved Dahlia.

Shhh, shhit. Beep, beep. Fffuck. Dahlia ducked her head, dripping tears, and pushed past us.

*　*　*

None of us wanted Dahlia in our lane, to be stuck next to her, waiting for the red second hand of the giant white plastic time clock that sat on the deck to hit its mark. If she spoke to you, the other girls might misinterpret this as conversation, as a budding friendship. Jessie, always keeping an eye on us. Out for us.

So, we left too early during intervals to catch up with Dahlia and grab at her ankles, throwing off her stroke. Spread out along the ledge at the wall so she'd have to cling to the lane line or tread water. Blocked off any extra room on the benches with our towels, flannel pants, gym bags. Forced her to sit with the boys or retreat into the locker room. Refused to speak to or cheer for her when we got stuck with her on a relay.

It didn't matter that she was fast.

Dahlia avoided changing in the open locker room with the rest of us. Our bodies still lean from childhood and growing sleeker from hours of weekly practice combined with height spurts to make us flashy fish. We couldn't help but look at each other. Steal glances. Compare shapes. Try out our best humblebrag—complain about our belly so someone else would praise it and disparage her own. Dahlia still had the kind of fat that only gets complimented by old ladies looking at a newborn.

Jill, a slight, mousy girl who'd only avoided Jessie's condescension by being so meek and inconsequential as to seem nonthreatening, tried to be nice to Dahlia in a quiet, don't-get-noticed way because her parents—devout Evangelical Christians—insisted that she demonstrate her love for Jesus by rooting for underdogs and befriending outcasts. A cruel standard at that age. On nights when she thought Dahlia might cry from Jessie's tormenting, Jill pretended to have to pee and slipped into the half-height concrete stall next to Dahlia's. Stared straight ahead, leaning against the short barrier. Ignored the clothes draped over the wall, a vicious reminder of why she should have stayed over by the maroon metal lockers.

Good job in that last set, Jill would whisper. Or, *I'll bet you do great in the meet this weekend*. She never mentioned the teasing or talked about anything personal.

She couldn't afford to like Dahlia.

*   *   *

Jessie stuffed the lavender cotton underwear into a toilet and flushed as the rest of us crowded around. She left the matching training bra dangling over the seat into the bowl. As the water gurgled toward the rim, she inventoried who of us laughed, who fidgeted.

"If she'd just stop embarrassing herself, we wouldn't need to do this," Jessie admonished, like a parent justifying spanking to the child she beat. "We can't have a freak on our team, right Jill?"

Jill nodded, eyes cast down to the tile still smelling of bleach from an earlier cleaning.

Dahlia hesitated when Jessie, wrapped in a neon-pink bath towel, leaned sideways next to her locker.

"Why don't you just quit?" she whispered as Dahlia shuffled through her bag, again and again, tics and hiccoughs and swears increasing with her panic. "If you would just learn to control yourself, Dahl, we wouldn't feel like you were insulting us. We want to help you, little miss piggy."

"Where, where—*beeeep, shit*—is my underwear? *Fuck!*" Dahlia bit down hard on her lip as she searched our semicircled faces for an ally.

"We left it in your changing room, Dahl," said Nicole, a strawberry-blond who lived in Duck Lake, a planned community in which every foyer rose three stories, crowned by a custom chandelier, and each bedroom featured a private bath. "Since you're too good to undress with the rest of us."

Dahlia didn't cry. Just involuntarily swore, grabbed her things, and fast-blinked her way out of the locker room. Jessie, who already had her own cell phone—just one more confirmation of her superiority—snapped a picture of Dahlia's pants soaked through from the swimsuit underneath. Posted online in seconds.

After that night, Dahlia came to practice already in her swimsuit. Her mother waiting in the second-floor cheering balcony with a change of clothes. In the hallway, Jill overheard Dahlia's mother insisting that they go to the coaches.

Beeping and hiccoughing, Dahlia hissed, "No! *Shit, shhhhit!* It's no big deal, Mom!"

*   *   *

Jessie continued her campaign, Nicole rising ranks to second-in-command, Amanda jealous but hiding it as best she could. The rest of us too scared to suggest backing off, even as we understood that we might, one day, look back and regret our behavior.

Every time Dahlia walked near enough, Jessie or Nicole reached out and snapped her swimsuit straps. Bright red lines like whipping wounds peeked from below the fabric. Amanda yanked off Dahlia's cap during rest intervals, hoping to catch hair. Leaving her to tread water and she stretched the cap back on, missing part of the set.

Knowing that Coach was watching out, as best as he could, for Dahlia at the behest of her parents, we timed our transgressions carefully. When he was preoccupied by the age group above us and a few lanes over, we took our shots. While he gave instructions to the high-school team in the dry-lands room, perfect opportunity. We complained to the older swimmers who ran Saturday practices about Dahlia swearing and laughed as they—having not been warned—took her aside for a scolding. We edged her out of team cheers or stopped in the middle of the yelling so her voice would ring out alone, then shook our heads at her embarrassment, as if pitying her. Spread rumors to the boys' team about her particular piggy smell.

When Jessie saw Jill talking to Dahlia on deck after a grueling practice, she grabbed their water bottles from the side of the pool and motioned us to follow.

"What's this? A freak of the week meeting? Careful, Jill. You might catch Tourette's."

"Leave, *fuck!* Leave her alone!" *Beep, beep.*

"You need this potty-mouth piggy to protect you, Jill?" laughed Nicole.

Jessie held out the water bottles. She pulled off the caps and bent toward the drain at the edge of the pool. Hair and scum clogged the grate. Spit and piss and traces from all the plantar-wart covered feet.

"Who's first?" She dragged the spouts of Dahlia's purple bottle and Jill's orange bottle along the edge, scraping hard enough to scratch the plastic and catch the grime, gathering up the warm chlorine. She shoved the bottles into their hands. "Drink up, ladies."

Dahlia refused first. Jessie feigned shock and stared at each of the girls, then began circling, the rest of us falling into a vulture perimeter. Jill wrung her hands, staring into the stands, perhaps praying for parental intervention or simply checking to see if the adults had left the building to wait outside in their warm station wagons.

"What are we going to do about our little Dahl?" Jessie mocked.

Jill reached out and rammed the purple bottle into Dahlia's mouth. Squeezed. "We'll feed our Dahl her bottle."

We laughed in revulsion, like watching a kid eat a worm on a dare. What else could we do?

"I guess you're not too thirsty, Jill." Jessie grinned as she took away the orange bottle and threw it into the on-deck trash can. "Let's go get Dahl some soap so she can wash out her potty mouth."

Dahlia vomited into the trash basket as we walked away. We left her swearing between sobs as we entered the locker room. We all silently thanked our luck that Dahlia's disorder and weight made her an easier target than our own acne and awkwardness made us.

*   *   *

Dahlia took first place in three individual events at Winter Championships. Set a team record for eleven- and twelve-year-old girls in the one-hundred-yard breaststroke. No one but our coaches cheered at the end of her lane. Jessie intentionally disqualified the relay she shared with Dahlia by false-starting. Nicole dumped her red sports drink on the crotch of Dahlia's team warm-up pants.

"Learn to use a tampon," she snickered for the rest of the afternoon. Most of us hadn't gotten our period yet and understood it to be something publicly shameful, even as we secretly hoped it would arrive soon. Before our younger sisters. Before every girl but us had turned into a woman.

As the year-end semiformal awards banquet approached, Coach gathered us in the gymnasium. Instead of swimming, we played team-building games. Trust falls, the human knot. We watched a scratchy VHS tape of girls in bright sweaters and sideways ponytails telling stories of pain caused by bullying. Coach nodded along and gave us his sternest look before releasing us to our parents.

Jessie abruptly eased up. When Amanda reached for Dahlia's straps, Jessie blocked her and snapped Amanda's instead. She pushed Nicole's purple Speedo duffel bag to the floor during the Zones meet in neighboring Indiana, making space for Dahlia to sit, placing her arm around the uncertain girl's shoulders. Sharing an earbud from her iPod. We watched, ever wary of Jessie's mercurial mood, wondering what was actually behind the sudden shift. Uncertain of our own behavior in light of the developments.

"Each season, at the banquet, I give a special gift to my best friend on the team," Jessie announced to Dahlia during an explanation of the upcoming awards ceremony. We all nodded, solemn, trying to appear interested but not eager. Not desperate. Jealous that we'd dropped in hierarchy in the recent weeks.

"That's n-n-nice—*shit, beep*—nice."

"Last year, Jessie gave me a gift certificate for us to go to any movie I chose," bragged Angela, a tall brunette who hunched over to hide her rapidly growing chest. She'd fallen from favor following a sleepover during when Jessie revealed a crush on Angela's older brother David, also a swimmer. Later in the night, the boy refused to kiss Jessie despite his sister's prodding. At practice the next day, Jessie marched over to the teen who'd first tried to tease her and whispered to him about David's *queerness*. A week later, Coach sat the older swimmers down for a talk about inappropriate language and the use of slurs.

"The season before that, she gave me her favorite necklace," chirped Amanda.

"This year, though, will be the best present yet," Jessie proclaimed, arm around Dahlia. "Only someone who's proven she won't betray me could deserve such a good gift."

Dahlia looked hopeful for the first time since joining the team. Like she might, finally, belong. She beeped, trying to cover her cursing.

"Let it out, girl." Jessie smiled. "We won't bite."

* * *

We met in the locker room before the awards banquet. Amanda and Jessie brought makeup and insisted on shadowing all of our eyes. Passed around lip gloss to make us adult pouty. Our new dresses from the juniors' rack at local department stores barely met the arbitrary hem length our mothers insisted on. Jill's parents wouldn't let her out of the house in anything above the knee, but they caved and allowed spaghetti straps as long as she wore a cardigan. In front of the mirrors, she shrugged off the sweater.

"I dare you to leave it in here when we go out to the tables!" Nicole pushed. Jill considered it, enjoying our nodding and attention.

Dahlia arrived last, wearing a swishy, sleeveless peach dress with fabric petals across the bodice. Her arms and legs, more toned than we'd realized. Jessie's eyes flashed with jealousy before calming.

"Oh my god, your dress is so pretty," she squealed. We chimed in with praises. "Come over here, let me do your eyes!" Jessie swiped gold shadow over Dahlia's lids, brushed on mascara, then held her by the shoulders as she stood back to admire her work. We all agreed that it was perfect.

Jessie led us to the horseshoe of wooden benches in the middle row of lockers and insisted we sit.

"This season is an *extra special* season, so I'm going to give out gifts to *all* of my best friends, instead of picking just one." We eyed her and each other, legs jittering, lips pursing as she walked around the inside of the semicircle. Watching us, she took on a reflective tone. "As you know, there is no greater expression of friendship than a friendship bracelet. I spent this whole month weaving them in special colors for my very best friends."

Jessie stopped pacing in front of Nicole and passed her a purple, white, and gold knotted bracelet with a raised ridge that swirled around the center. Nicole gasped and slipped it on. "It's beautiful!" She beamed at each of us, holding up her wrist.

Next, Amanda received a chevron pattern in turquoise, cerulean, and black. "It fits perfectly!" she exclaimed. Jessie kissed her cheek.

Angela got an orange, yellow, and crimson fishtail. Other girls got ones with tiny translucent beads or pink and black dots. Jill's bracelet featured lavender hearts with a sage background, and she looked at Jessie in shock.

"Of course you're one of my best friends, Jill. Don't you know how much I adore you?"

Jill looked down at her wrist with a small smile.

As Jessie walked around the circle, we compared our bracelets while waiting to see who of the remaining girls would get one, too. The more she gave out, the less special each one felt, and we tried to hide our disappointment. With four girls to go, only three more bracelets dangled from Jessie's wrist and we thought we knew what was coming. She'd been planning this all along.

"Almost all of my best friends have a symbol of our friendship now!" Jessie held up her own braceleted wrist to show off the most colorful threads. She turned to look at Dahlia, the only girl left with nothing for her arm. "Oh sweetie, don't cry, you'll ruin your mascara. You don't think I've forgotten you, do you?"

Dahlia hiccoughed.

"Since you're my very *bestest* friend, I wanted to do something extra special for you. Your bracelet is waiting for you in the dry-lands room. With Brian."

We gasped. Everyone knew Dahlia had a crush on Brian, the hottest guy in the thirteen and fourteen age group. We all had a crush on him. Jessie beamed and nudged Dahlia toward the door as we cooed jealously.

"Enjoy, darling. And don't take too long, or you'll miss the awards. We'll save you a seat."

We shuffled out of the locker room, some of us lingering briefly, wondering whether we should follow Dahlia. Not knowing if it would make things better or worse.

Out in the high-school cafeteria, we sat ourselves around circular tables covered in maroon-and-gold tablecloths and spread our beaded purses to the sides, barring anyone from sliding up an extra chair. A gaggle of boys walked into the room in blazers and loosened ties, hair slightly disheveled. Laughing. One of them high-fived Brian, who winked at Jessie.

Dahlia emerged fifteen minutes later, her dress bodice missing a few of its petals. She darted puffy eyes around the room. Her parents offered an enthusiastic wave, but she ignored them as she walked toward us, mutterings increasing in frequency and volume as she scanned and rescanned our faces. Each of us thinking, perhaps, that we should let her sit with us. That Jessie didn't have to be so mean. That maybe something bad had happened, something worse than scummy water or relentless teasing.

"Where's your bracelet, piggy? I spent a lot of time making it extra special for you," Jessie hissed when Dahlia reached her side. She snickered at her teammate. "You didn't actually think I really liked you, did you?"

Dahlia walked over to the front-most table and sat alone, on display, with the parents and other athletes behind her. Seven barren folding chairs kept her company for the evening. Jill hesitated but saw Jessie's raised eyebrow. When a few of our mothers came over to whisper in our ears—*Don't you think you should invite that poor girl to sit with you?*—we brushed them away.

It's not our fault, we justified. *She's gross, Mom.* Our mothers backed off, not wanting their own daughters cast out by association. At least they made a show of being considerate, they reasoned. They could talk to us later, at home, where the only repercussions we'd face would be their admonitions. Maybe a light punishment designed to teach us about empathy.

We tried to ignore the sound of Dahlia's parents sniffling back tears as they watched their daughter eat chicken fettucine alfredo alone. Receive her "rookie of the year" award in front of a silent girls' team. Sit back down unsmiling.

We told ourselves we were doing the right thing. The safe thing.

*   *   *

Years later, after it all happened, we would watch our own children wrestle through the vicious dynamics of adolescence. Wonder at how much we ought to intervene. We would ache for our offspring to be better than we were, kinder. But we would ache, too, for them to be spared the anguish of not belonging.

*   *   *

She did it on purpose. She must have.

One of the first things we learned as young swimmers: surface-diving. How to slice the top water and skim our bodies through the first layer. Dahlia was the best off the blocks every time. The shallow end was nearly four feet deep.

When she walked out of the locker room on the first night of summer practice, we began our snickering. Nicole reached for a strap. Dahlia slapped away her hand.

"Fuck you!" Clearly, calmly, not lurching it out. We wondered later if she practiced for hours that afternoon in front of her bedroom mirror. She strode over to Jessie and stood, staring, until Jessie started taunting her.

"Potty-mouth piggy, didn't learn her less—"

Dahlia shoved her into the pool. Jessie surfaced and began shouting, clutching her arm where it scraped the lane line. Down at the other end, Coach turned to see what caused the ruckus. Amanda moved to grab Dahlia, but Dahlia ducked her hand and pushed her across the deck. Amanda slipped and fell on her tailbone. The rest of us stood back, stunned.

"What are you waiting for? That slut shoved me. Throw that bitch in the water!" yelled Jessie as she hoisted herself out of the pool. We froze as Coach began fast-walking toward the scene, taking careful steps so he wouldn't slip on the slick deck.

Dahlia turned to Jill and mouthed *sorry*. Walked to the edge of the shallow end, curled her toes around the white-and-maroon tiles. Dahlia's mother began screaming in the stands as soon as her daughter blew a kiss and shut her eyes.

Dahlia jumped slightly and dove straight for the bottom, hands tucked by her sides. Hit her head in the center of the black stripe that lined the pool floor. She barely splashed.

The coaches, trained as lifeguards, panicked at the possible spinal injury and argued over how to use the backboard properly. They debated whether to risk paralysis by yanking her out of the water or to move her only enough to bring her head above the surface. Dahlia's mother continued screaming, even as the paramedics later half-carried her out to the ambulance to ride along.

We sat thigh to thigh on the benches to which they shuffled us after she dove. Our swim caps were still on, goggles tucked into the edges of our suits. We watched our teammate, immobile, on an orange plastic board, as our coaches held her hands. Silently cursed Dahlia for leaving us vulnerable.

We cursed ourselves, for being so shallow.

"Wow. Didn't think she had it in her." Jessie, bundled in a towel after her unexpected dip, smirked down the bench. "Must be hard for you, Jill. I mean, you two were close, right?"

We laughed, tentatively tugging at our bracelets.

KATE BUCCA holds an MFA from Vermont College of Fine Arts and a BFA from Goddard College. Her work has appeared in DigBoston, The Nervous Breakdown, Welter, Glass, The Tishman Review, and elsewhere. She teaches humanities at a small school in New Jersey, where she lives with the writer Dominic Bucca and two cats, Snack and Barney.

Lida

Belal Rafiq

I took home a pregnant girl. I first saw her on the bleachers in
Esquire Park. She watched the boys by the iron Mirdad monument fight kites over the lawn. Her hair brushed the cerulean dress
that waterfalled over her belly and exposed her pale calves. She
swung her sandaled feet, sometimes stretching them out like she
needed to know they were still there. No one sat with her.

Fall was starting, and we park custodians patrolled the paths,
not giving a leaf a chance to touch the ground. They armed us
with aluminum trash pickers, black plastic boots, and yellow jump-
suits. You could spot a rookie by how their unwashed bright outfits
gleamed in the sun.

We found our own figure-eight routines that covered the park,
and picked up all of the Styrofoam plates and kabob aluminum
foil we could. Whenever Masood and I met on the paths, we'd
raise our pickers high and pull back on the handles, trying to clamp
the rubber tips together in unity. Sometimes, his arm would be
up and he'd jerk forward to clamp my balls, but he stopped that
the day after I bent his picker in half and chucked it in the pond.
The supervisor should've yelled at me but didn't because I was never
trouble. I got a laugh out of Masood saying, "Shit, if it was summer,

I would've dove in after that shit, and you would've been all jealous of my ass in the water."

The later shifts were better because the sun weakened after three, and I didn't have to pick up the beer bottles and condoms that ornamented the corner holly bushes in the mornings. The ones leaving those were always sober enough to pile their shit where the old couldn't see. Kept the park innocent for them.

Late afternoons, Potomac air invaded the east side and snaked through the trees. I'd catch the breezes in my collar because they bubbled my suit like a falling skydiver's.

Vendors closed their carts at dusk and Masood always wanted me to ask for the leftover scraps they would throw away.

"C'mon, Nabil. People don't like me," he told me the first time. "You got that, like, noble knight shit about you."

I held the picker above my head like victory.

"And you're tall."

"What's that got to do with it?"

"You can impose on a motherfucker."

"So if nice doesn't work, I can intimidate a gyro out of a tired—"

"You've got nice hair."

"I'm not that tall."

"You've got better Dari skills."

"Look, just—"

"People like you more than me, all right?" he said, because I saved money, said *salaam* with a smile, and had vendors' wives asking me why I'm thirty and not married. "Because I'm waiting for you to leave your husband," I always told them. They knew my dad when he was alive, and were sure I inherited his kind heart.

* * *

I told Masood I'd see him later and he followed the path out, guiding a lost old couple to the exit. I saved the bleachers for last because they stood by the paths that lead home. It was close to nine and the pregnant girl was still there. The girl took something from a black bag too big to be a purse, and leaned back. My picker was caught on a loose screw in the metal jungle under her seat, and when I pulled, the picker slammed into one of the hollow steel pillars, echoing something like a laser blast.

"Sorry," I said, coming out. "Hope I didn't, y'know, scare you."

"It's okay," she promised, leaning back again, smiling, palms on her belly. The glow of the lamps shadowed most of her face.

I turned and walked a few steps, but came back. "You know it might not be safe around here at night," I said to her. "I mean it's safe, but the lamps don't hit here and it's dark—"

"Aren't you tired?" she asked, turning to me.

"Hm?"

"You've been picking up trash all day, I've seen you. You emptied your bag three times."

"I don't remember seeing you eat. I can get you some food. You want water?"

"You were watching me too?"

"Well, yeah. Worried. Who leaves their girl—"

"Whose parents kick their six-month pregnant daughter out?"

Baba would kick my ass for not helping her. I was nice, but he was goodness incarnate. If you were a rained-drenched salesman or delivery boy, he'd pull you into the apartment fast like a tidal wave was gonna eat you in the hallway. The strangers always said they could wait in the building lobby, but Baba insisted on tea and blankets. He was so genuine and pushy that he made a few stragglers take showers, while guess who had to dive sixteen floors to the laundry room and wash a strange dude's drawers? Using salad tongs to dump the clothes, I boiled inside knowing that a naked stranger could be stealing our shit and getting away with it—Baba was too swollen and chip-hipped to chase anybody; it took him half a painful minute to turn around. Maybe that's why nobody stole anything. Baba's seahorse posture could make the homeless feel sorry for him.

* * *

When Lida wasn't gripping my wrist coming down the bleachers or up the steps in the park, she said nothing; just held her big purse bag below her stomach where she could feel it punching her thin thighs. Two more months of baby on her frame, and she'd have to limbo-walk not to fall on her face.

At home, she noticed I had mattresses instead of couches, and no dining table.

"Kandahārī?" she asked.

"Yup." She looked Panjshiri, from her light hair and eyes.

"Pashto?"

"Dari."

"How come?"

"Okay, there's a bathroom in your room, but if you want to take a shower, there's the one in the hall."

"Okay," she said. "It's like an art gallery with no art. Don't worry, that's not a bad thing. Just a thing thing."

"I can warm up some *palauw*, or give you some extra blankets if you want."

She slowly spun around. "Which room is it that—"

"End of the hall." The four-foot hall.

I waited until the lights went off under her door (Baba's old room) to take a shower. Pregnant women, I thought, had to keep eating or drinking, and she was doing too little of both. Maybe she was trying to put me on the line for something, and that this whole thing is a setup for her and her husband to sue the green out of a dumb shit. My money stayed in a safe in my room, and it would've sucked to spend it on the crap results of good intentions. She couldn't stay for long.

At 4 a.m., a heavy-heeled marching punished the linoleum in the kitchen. I woke with my hands in my hair while I burned my feet roughing through the carpet. The lights were off and I saw a figure absorbing the light of the fridge. Lida's elbow was high in the air as milk dripped down her neck and into the same dress she wore at the park. She saw me and choked. She put the milk back in, closed the fridge, and wiped her chin, wrist to elbow.

"I thought I found the light, but the switch didn't do anything, so I couldn't find a cup," she said. "I tried to drink it without putting my lips on it, but I kept missing my mouth. Some got in my nose. I thought I was gonna drown," she chuckled. White pooled around her toes. "I'll clean it up. Promise."

I released the test button on the wall switch. "Should work now, just don't hit that button again," I said. "You can use the clothes in your room if you need to change."

*   *   *

In the morning, she laid out butter, long Afghan bread, honey, toast, smelly cheeses, and rainbow jellies on the floor in front of the two mattresses. Lida had puzzled together all of my placemats to protect the carpet.

"Salaam!" she beamed, touching her cheeks to mine and kissing the air. She dressed in Baba's old undershirts and nylon sweats. They made good maternity wear.

"Salaam," I said, trying to rub out the magnetic strands on the back of my head.

"Nice breakfast before work," she claimed.

"Did you go out and get these?"

"I had some extra money. I had to wait for somebody to let me in the building, though." That meant that she left my door unlocked.

"Here, I'll pay you back." I went to my room and she followed, protesting. She braked in my doorway.

"Your room is like the rest of your house," she said.

"Yeah." I kept my back to her so she couldn't see the combo on the safe. "What'd you expect?"

"I don't know," she shrugged, sliding inside, balancing herself with the wall so she could sit on my bed—the mattress on the floor. "People's rooms are different than their living rooms. But my room has a bed frame, and nightstands."

"It's the guest room."

"You don't have any paintings or posters or pictures in yours."

"I have memories," I said, holding out a few folded twenties.

"You don't need to pay me back," she said. Her eyes sharpened, "That looks like more—"

"There's a little extra."

"Little extra?"

"For you, you might need it," I said. "For a hotel."

"Can we just, just eat first?" Her eyebrows straightened, and her mouth twitched like it was holding a frown back. I was defenseless to how she made me villainous. I dropped the money on the mattress, and she led me back to the living room like I'd never been there before.

I spent half of the conversation scraping the burns off the toast, and she spent the other half apologizing and praising my strong oven.

"You're the only Afghan ever with no toaster," she said.

She told me she lived on the north side of the island where the houses were. Her parents kept her at home when her belly started to show, and told her to stay in the house until the baby was born. They thought that as long as Lida was seen without a pregnant belly, no one in the neighborhood would ask questions. When they found out she was sneaking the car to midnight movie showings in Burke, they threw her out.

"I don't really blame them," Lida said. "I'm not married and I'm pregnant. They don't know how to explain that to other people. They play strong and don't bring up any weaknesses."

"That how you think it is?" I said, looking at her arms, thinking that her parents didn't feed her. Unless it was genetics.

"They told me to go back to the *gookhor* who did this to me."

A Persian guy who worked the sunglass stand by the restaurant she served at. She said he was more pretty than handsome, and was too small to be as loud as he was. When the doctor confirmed she was with child, she never went to work again. She never knew where he lived.

*　*　*

Masood believed her less than I did.

"Are you sure she doesn't have a pillow under her shirt?" he asked. "I mean, have you seen her shirtless? Okay, maybe not, but have you seen her in a tight shirt? Like a size small from the teen section?"

"She's twenty-four," I said.

"You should've gave her your white tee and been like: 'oh my goodness, I just spilled like a whole glass of water all over your stomach.' Then you'd know."

"I can't tell if you're joking."

"Wait, did she leave?"

"I told her she could stay one more night." That was true.

"You left her alone at your place?"

"What am I supposed to do?"

"Not leave a stranger—"

"She's alone."

"She doesn't have parents here, Nab. I'm telling you. It's bullshit. She came here and got knocked up."

I didn't care if she lied about her past, as long as everything else was the truth.

*　　*　　*

Lida simmered potatoes and I put a bag down by the counter. She bought a rice cooker and a toaster with the money that was on my bed. I should've been angry.

"Shopping?" she asked from only hearing the bags. "Fun." She had one hand on her hip, and one stirring the pot. One of Baba's longsleeves was tied over her stomach, and her hair stood proud in a bun. She looked like she knew where everything in the kitchen was. I knew the longer she stayed, the sooner I'd fall for her.

"Did you go to the Southside?" I asked.

"Took the bus."

"The bus."

"The. Bus."

*　　*　　*

"When's your next doctor's appointment?" I asked at dinner. She used her first three fingers to scoop rice into her mouth. I'd only seen older folks do that.

"Couple weeks," she mumbled, while some things tumbled off her lips.

"Think your parents are worried? Think they started asking around or something?"

She pointed a glistening finger at me. "You're worried about getting in trouble? People knowing I'm here?"

"I mean, they probably thought you were gonna go to a friend's house for a day and come back."

She smiled. "I'm not at a friend's house right now?"

I went to the kitchen and brought the bag. "Here."

She put her bowl down and wiped her hands on the shirt-apron. Stray grains of rice stuck to her lap. "Vitamins!"

"Calcium and folic acid. Did some reading last night."

"Reading? For me?"

"They sold out of iron, so I'll go back tomorrow."

"Tomorrow?" she sang.

"Tomorrow."

That night she called me into her room, and she was under the covers, on her side, with a gray t-shirt collar darkening between her teeth. She was embarrassed to ask for more pillows. She wanted to see if sleeping upright would help her back. This meant that I had to give her my pillows and sleep flat-backed like Baba did when I was a kid. Every morning that I burst into his room, I'd find fluffy casualties against the door, beaten like they tried to escape. I used to think that was his way of telling me to stay out, so I beat him with those pillows until he woke up or gave up.

"You can stay," Lida said. "If you want."

"You have a boyfriend."

"He never was my boyfriend. And I don't want him to be."

In my bed, sleeping without pillows meant a corkscrew-necked morning and an afternoon of not being able to look up. Baba's mattress was a king-size softy. I told her that I would stay because she might need something else in the middle of the night.

She woke up three times for the bathroom, and landed back on bed, nestling closer and closer to me until we kissed, her belly a hot barrier between us.

*   *   *

Baba's blue shirt hovered over Lida's bare thighs as she flipped hash browns. She slapped my hands with the stirrer when I tried help, so I put my arms around her, smelling and listening to the food sizzle.

"You're always making potatoes," I said.

"Cravings. Pregnant."

"Aren't you cold?"

"Nope."

I couldn't interlock my fingers, so I put them below her belly, and lifted it a little like it would take some weight off of her. She giggled and leaned back, landing a long one on my scruff, not telling me I need to shave.

On my way out, I told her to take her vitamins.

She rushed at me and pinched my chin. "Hey, mister, who's the parent here?"

*   *   *

Petting-zoo weekend was once a month depending on the weather. Farmers came from the south and the west on short trucks the length of two parking spaces. Park workers were responsible for dragging the plastic logs from the back of the office out to the fields. Unless you were new, you didn't need the instruction booklets to make the barriers. Farmers brought haystacks to wall in the smaller animals, and they sometimes brought kiddie pools for people to buy goldfish. I guarded the small-animals pen with an old-lady farmer. We watched one mother, scarved beyond comfort, pet a guinea pig with her finger and twitch away like it scolded her. Her daughter picked the animal up and fed it a pellet. On these days, the kids were the brave ones.

Lida surprised me with a hug and I looked over her to see if anyone I knew was looking. I hadn't seen Masood yet. She wore clear lipstick and one of Baba's bright blue V-necks. I jerked away when she tried to kiss me.

"I smell bad. You don't want none of this," I said.

"Okay." She shrugged her shoulders and looked at the pony-ride station. "You know how to make a pony cry?"

"How?" I asked.

"You put me on his back," she smiled, going into my pen.

"You're not heavy," I said to her back. She sat on a crate and massaged the top of a baby goat's head with her fingers. A bunny ate the grass around her feet as Lida cupped a fuzzy golden chick. She brought it to me by the gate and I stared at the bird as it was brought closer and closer to my face. It pecked my nose, and I flinched. Lida hid her laugh behind her hands and popped out to kiss me when I tucked my big embarrassed head.

* * *

A week later, Masood invited us to dinner so he could meet her. When we knocked on his door, he slid out, holding the door tight like he was hiding a murder.

"We're going to my mom's," he said. I looked at Lida in her new green dress, matching eyes, and light-plum lipstick. "Don't worry," Masood said, "I told her you guys were cousins."

"Really? My cousin who's pregnant and came to visit me *alone*."

"I live in Dumfries with my husband who's away on work," Lida said. "I stay with my parents in Fairfax until he comes back in a couple weeks."

"See that? Girl's good." Masood said to me.

"What if she sees you around like a month from now?" I asked her.

"Hm, what if?" she hummed against my cheek. Masood crossed his arms and puffed.

I loved his mom, but POWs wouldn't eat her food. Khala Vohra had high sodium and decided that everyone else did too. She tried every salt substitute: when she tried lemon, my jaw hurt and I had to speak with my neck like a German; with cayenne, fire dragoned out of my ass and my throat burned for two days. One month, she used MSG and I was excited she finally found her cooking groove, but I broke down and told her what the initials stood for. She cursed the world for taking a victory from her, and Masood arced the can into the trash. To him, her food wasn't crap, just not as good as all the other food he ever had in his life.

She collected rugs, and laid them on the floor so thick that her apartment was ten degrees hotter and an extra three inches above sea level. I sometimes tripped on the rug flaps when I stepped out of her normal-level kitchen, and only wished I fell when a pot of her beef was in my hands. I would've gladly taken the burns.

Our plate bottoms stuck to the plastic tablecloth, so bringing your plate closer meant bringing everyone else's. It was like playing ouija.

* * *

Lida was welcomed with a graspy happiness that made her look like family. Khala Vohra's bubbly soda voice controlled all pleasant conversation. I was surprised that she couldn't get enough of Lida. But the fake backstory was too detailed to be fake. I couldn't verify some of the answers. Was she really born in Weslaco, Texas? Did her father really punch a communist? Shit, did she really have a husband? Truth or lie, Lida's Dari didn't stutter, it was slow, calculated, better than mine. Khala eventually took her to the bedroom to show her some homeland photos of when she herself was pregnant.

Lida hadn't flinched when she ate the beef *mantu*, but every overspiced dumpling was a battle down my throat—I drank enough water to swallow a bowling ball.

"So what's it like fucking a pregnant girl?" Masood said plainly.

"What'd you say?" I wiped my mouth.

"I mean, do you have to hit it from the back the whole time? There's probably no face to face huh?"

"How do you say some shit like that to me?"

"Nab, what's gonna happen when that baby's born?"

"Whatever's gonna happen."

"'Whatever's gonna happen.' Dumbass, you don't know her, it's not your kid."

"I should dump her on the street, that's what I should do."

"You can't raise a baby."

"I've got money saved up," I said, going back to work on my plate.

"That how she got the dress? That how she gonna get other dresses? And baby food? Wipes? Diapers? Cradles? Fucking strollers? Are you sure someone's not looking for her?"

"I've got money saved up."

"I love you, Nab, but—"

"Masood?" His eyes were red and holding.

"You deserve someone perfect."

"Thanks, thanks. You do too."

"No. You? You're a good guy, you're a better man than I am."

*   *   *

Lida woke with a fever in the morning, so I took a sick day. I filled the tub halfway with cold water. She leaned her back against my chest and her belly islanded out of the water. For hours, I played with her long fingers and slowly clawed her belly and legs. She fell asleep whenever the water warmed.

The nausea and throwing up didn't scare me until the next day. In the morning, I saw her shiver from the bedroom to the tub, and called out of work again. I tried to give her some crackers and ginger ale to calm her stomach, but nothing stayed down. Her neck ached and the water took less and less time to warm. Lida cried every time I felt her forehead. Sometimes we'd sit up and hold each other, me repeating, "It's just the flu." I knew it wasn't that or food poisoning, because I kissed her, and spent moments inside her, hoping to get sick, but my body stayed quiet. When you're pregnant, the only thing more dangerous than a contagious problem is noncontagious one.

"I'll leave if you call a doctor," she said plainly.

"You have to go."

"I'll get better."

"You're getting worse."

"Just a little longer."

"You keep saying that."

"Save your money."

I climbed out of the tub and stormed through the cold blitz. I came back dry and dressed.

"If we don't go now," I commanded, taking my phone out. "I'm gonna *spend money* on an ambulance."

Watching her get up was seeing her in old age. She clutched my forearm and I held her above her elbows so she could slide her wrinkly feet out.

* * *

Masood drove us to the hospital. Lida had a listeria infection, and they took her to testing rooms I wasn't allowed into.

"I hope the baby's okay," Masood attempted.

"No shit," I said, staring at a weird poster of a doctor posing like a wizard, a needle in his pocket.

Khala Vohra sat across from me and asked over and over if I wanted something from the cafeteria. She never mentioned Lida's husband. She never asked why no other family members came by during the three days Lida was in the hospital. Lida lost the baby, and Khala stayed with her during my work shifts. The first day, I felt guilty about it, until I came into the room and the two stopped speaking. They greeted me all cordial, like I was the doctor.

When Lida and I were alone, she'd only speak when she needed a blanket or some pudding. She pleaded with the doctor to let her leave, but he wouldn't. She huffed about it costing me money, and I told her her words were useless. So she stopped talking to me.

Lida moved in with Khala Vohra one day after the hospital let her go. I know she would've gone earlier if she didn't spend her time washing Baba's clothes and saying goodbye. We hugged for five goddamn minutes.

* * *

During Halloween weekend, people pitched in to set up the haunted trails, outdoor fog machines, and black lights. I walked through the middle path in civilian clothes, and gave a wave to Masood, who was in a tree clearing the branches of toilet paper. The worker in the adjacent tree hooked fake spider webs on the leaves, and the cotton hung down like snot. I walked over to Masood.

"I know," he yelled from up high. "I've been watching him. He sucks."

"He new?" I yelled back.

"Yeah," he said.

"Well, I'm out."

"You're here for the morning shift tomorrow."

"I know."

"Have fun, Nab. I'll come later."

On the Southside of the island, the club line was long, but the entrance was still in sight. I checked out all of the out-of-towners with costumes and saw the back of Lida's head a few people ahead of me. I thought about calling out, then brushed off the idea. I would see her inside if I wanted to.

It took an hour to get in, and by the time I got a drink, Masood slapped me on the back, and begged me to find someone to dance with. The smells here even drowned him out.

I danced for two minutes and stepped off the floor. Masood rolled up his sleeves and extended his fists like someone was supposed to fit him with armor. He started this tornado move, turning faster and faster. The orange lights lit him up like fire, and the people rippled away in fear, but he kept spinning and spinning.

BELAL RAFIQ *grew up in the D.C. Metro Area. He received is MFA from Columbia University, where he was a Fiction Fellow. He was an Emerging Writer's Fellow at the Center for Fiction, and has fiction forthcoming in The Iowa Review. He currently lives in Brooklyn, and is working on a collection of stories.*

Quiet Guest

Dawna Kemper

M iranda stood in her closet, a space snug as an upright coffin, which was not a comparison she wanted to make but there it was. Though it was long past time to dress for work, she was still in her pajamas, determined to pry open the velvet necklace box in her hands, but her fingers were trembling and could not manage it, and she was on the verge of despair. The box was narrow, the latch impossibly stuck. She brought it to her mouth and like a trapped animal tried to bite it open, but that only hurt her teeth. The latch and hinges were gold, and the box was covered in royal blue velvet, the fabric showing its age though the warp still felt downy. It seemed childish, but she could not stop herself from petting it. She stroked the velvet and began to slide down the closet wall. As she sank, she wondered what her mother, across town, was doing—or undoing—in that very moment.

Inside the velvet box, her mother's pearls nestled in satin. She remembered the look of those pearls around her mother's neck, like tiny teeth feeding on her. The pearls were natural, and rare, recovered from the deep by expert pearl divers in Japan known as *ama*: "ocean women." Once, with her paycheck, Miranda bought herself a strand of her own pearls which she wore every day and without irony. For some time, she had believed that these pearls constituted her signature, because young women like her no longer wore an accessory so old-fashioned as daily pearls. Now, it seemed a ridiculous lie. Unlike her mother's natural pearls, the pearls Miranda could afford were cultured, which was an elegant way of saying they had been farmed. She regretted buying them at all. Now, she understood what it takes to produce a cultured pearl: a long needle must insert a foreign object into the oyster's soft insides. Bivalves are highly sensitive, and workers tasked with this job say the silent oysters flinch when pierced by the needle.

*   *   *

She was late again. Her teaching job was at an exclusive preschool where the children were precocious and pressured. These children had anxieties she understood, but which must surely be unnatural in four-year-olds. She hung her coat on a peg and rushed into the language-arts room. Her heels clicked too loudly on the tile, however much she tried to make them quieter. The clacking had a frank overtone that made her cringe. Her coteacher Victoria shot her a look, then continued on as if Miranda were not there. At the long low tables, the children's heads bowed over paper, crayons moving, their neural pathways quietly firing. On the board, Victoria was drawing an elaborate orchid in chalk of pale pink and delicate green. Victoria had an MFA in studio art from RISD; she was fluent in five languages including Farsi, Irish Gaelic, and Japanese. The orchid was luxuriant and fully formed. It swayed imperceptibly on the cold black board. The petals were lush and velvety even in chalk. Next to the orchid were graceful kanji, also alive, also quivering in their own silent, contained way. With a start, Miranda recognized that this subtle word for orchid also meant *quiet guest*. On a morning like this, it was a confluence of too much beauty. She stepped back, overwhelmed by it all. She opened her fists. Her chest felt like glass into which snow was gently falling. The room was so bright and so hushed she thought it might shatter her. She breathed in and gathered light in her lungs. The industrious children took no notice.

After she recovered, she felt stunned and weepy. Disoriented, she watched Victoria walk back and forth before the blackboard, saying something over and over in Japanese that she did not understand at all. She tried to get her bearings. A little girl who was new and struggling was seated nearby and she crouched next to her, gripping the back of the girl's chair to keep herself from toppling over. The little girl's name was Portia, and she wore a cashmere grass-green sweater. The girl was a half year older than the other children and this made her seem slow. Her hair was a blond shade just shy of transparent, and through the filaments of hair, Miranda could see the girl's pale scalp. Portia tried to make her crayon reproduce the kanji but the crayon kept sticking to the paper and veering off into crude skid marks. The girl's escalating fury and self-hatred were palpable. Miranda whispered in her ear: *wabi-sabi, wabi-sabi*. She quietly took the crayon from the girl's fingers and sharpened it. She turned over the paper to the side that was clean and blank, and she guided Portia's hand to begin forming the kanji's difficult turns. This was forbidden and she could now feel the full force of Victoria's glare boring into her. She would be written up again. But she could also feel Portia's thin shoulders relax. The little girl swallowed hard. She gripped the crayon and kept trying, and Miranda's throat unexpectedly knotted for this child she barely knew.

*   *   *

No one is more aware of her breath than an ama. An ocean woman sinking deep for pearls feels intimately the pliancy of her lungs as the currents press against her skin, ever alert to the balance between exertion and stillness. Breathing is one crucial lesson an ama passes on for her daughter's survival, to thwart the sea from smothering her girl: *Here is how you push deep without the blackness overcoming you; here is how you repel the sea when it longs to slip inside the delicate channels of your lungs.*

*   *   *

On the subway after work she stood sandwiched among a group of middle-school girls in uniforms. The girls were giggly and alive and conspiratorial. One girl popped the cap off a stubby red tube of lip gloss; she smeared her lips then handed it to the next girl who swiped the tube over her mouth. The tube passed from girl to girl, their lips freshly glistening. Miranda could not bear to look at them. She held onto the pole and let the subway rock her as it hurtled over the rails.

Hold on.

It is dark and it is deep.

The subway car smelled of burritos and urine and the girls' strawberry lip gloss. Concussive laughter startled her. These girls laughed with their mouths wide open, flashing pearl and silver and plump tongue. She was only ten years older, but she was an interloper. Their eyes were bright and hungry. They were impatient and keen. These were not yet girls who read Sylvia Plath and dreamed up myriad tragic ways of offing themselves. One girl was vigorously rimming her eyes with kohl; the pencil tugged at her pliant inner lid. When she finished and clicked away her mirror she caught Miranda looking. The girl stared back, her eyes a frank shock of blue through black smudge. Miranda glanced down at an old gum wrapper. She could feel the girl's scrutiny sweep over her, inspecting her top-drawer preschool teacher pumps, her skirt, her coat, her bag, her makeup, her neat ponytail. Her scalp tingled with heat. The subway rounded a curve and the kohl-eyed girl grabbed the pole. Her hand brushed Miranda's and the girl looked at her again, but this time the smudged eyes could not conceal the girl's shy embarrassment and this honest contact startled her. Just as quickly the girl looked away, and together they held on and leaned into the curve.

*   *   *

Miranda's mother was a stunner. Her eyes were purest green. Shocking glass green. Glamorous green. Inscrutable green. A cabbie once said, "No one has green eyes like that anymore." Her mother had looked away. Miranda was little then and she watched her mother's startled gaze dart around the cab like an exotic finch seeking a safe place to land, until at last her mother simply leaned back and closed her eyelids. She had put her open hand up to her mother's mouth; on her palm she could feel her mother's exhalation, warm and moist. The delicate rhythm of her mother's breath reassured her; she wanted the drive to continue forever, so the warm feeling would never cease. But when they abruptly pulled up at their building, her mother had opened the cab door and was pushing money into Miranda's hand for the fare and tip. She called out for her to wait, but her mother was already disappearing into the lobby, her perfect legs pale and moving beneath the dark hem of her coat. The cabbie was also watching her mother. She waited for him to notice the bills she held up in the air. When he finally took them, his fingers touched hers and she felt a jolt of shame. Before she fled after her mother, the cabbie winked at her.

*   *   *

In Japan, the ama are bare breasted and sleek as seals. Around their necks, in a large woven pouch, they secure a heavy stone. When they dive from the pier, the stone pulls them down through the water with little effort. The stone seeks the sea floor and drags the women with it. In this way, as they drop through the currents, the women reserve their energy for the task at hand, their nimble fingers ready to palpate the shy oysters. Later, they will need their strength to kick upward through the heavy moving sea, back toward light and air, their lungs empty, their baskets full.

*   *   *

She ascended the subway steps into a city twilight that turned the building facades dull violet. The streets were noisy and the air felt filmy in her mouth. She craned her neck and tried to see the sky. In the topmost rows of windows, the sun flashed gold for a few long moments then disappeared like a trick. People bumped roughly into her but she could not feel them in this dream. She searched the small patch of sky, pale and trapped. She was looking for something unnamable. There was the dread inside her but there was something outside her, too, that she recognized as a force that could not be stopped. She tried to sense whether the unstoppable thing she dreaded had happened. Or was still preparing to happen. Or was happening right now, somewhere not far from here. She brought her gloved hands to her face; she covered her face and her eyes, the leather cold on her eyelids. She tried to breathe deep, but her chest was so tight it hurt. In the dark behind her gloves, she strained to catch the very moment of her mother's death, to seize and mark it. But she feared that in this din of life the moment would escape her and pass like any other.

She tried, but there was nothing.

Her hands dropped back down to her sides. Around her, the city clamored.

The wind. She could feel the chilled wind on her face. That was all.

With effort, she tried to collect herself, but her eyes watered and she could not see. She pulled her coat tighter against the cold, and entered the flow of pedestrians, down the avenue toward the hotel.

*   *   *

The tiny island of Hegura—Hegurajima—is fleeting home to thousands of migratory birds, some plain, some beautiful, some meek, some bloodthirsty. On this island, the ama set out while the village is asleep to prepare themselves for the day's dive. In the early morning, they walk in silence through a swirling cloud of mist and fog, their cotton kimonos wrapped loosely about their bodies. The moist air dampens the fabric to their skin and they shiver. One woman leads the way with her lantern. Behind her, the girls move with swift, light steps; their mothers plant their feet firmly. Three elders, nearly a century old, follow with deliberation, arms linked for steadiness, but their legs remain stocky and strong. From the east, the ocean summons the women with its whisper. Up ahead, fog parts to reveal the low wooden hut, the *amagoya*, with its tile roof. When they reach its threshold, one young woman bows to the others and enters first to prepare the fire. At the doorway, another woman holds the lantern high while the girls and women part to make way for the three elders. They enter, one by one, and gather around the shrine next to the fire. As the women remove their kimonos, a sustained bellow swells from somewhere deep in the sea. The sound is haunting and plaintive. The cry fills the hut and the women exchange looks. They know it is the beast that slumbers deep beneath the water's surface; he lurks in the shadows of the deepest oyster beds where the finest pearls may be found. Many years ago, one of the elders narrowly escaped it. The demon has black shiny scales; its fangs are long and yellow, its talons dirty and sharp, and once it latches on to you its grip is inescapable. In its forehead are three luminous eyes that hypnotize any diver careless enough to look into them. One woman says: "It is lonely this morning." Another replies: "It wants a wife." But as they begin to prepare their bodies with grease, slicking their skin for the dive ahead, the women are unafraid. They have each other.

*   *   *

In a room overlooking the city, on a silk divan, a woman wakes from a long slumber. Her green eyes flutter open. Slowly, she pushes her body upright, pats her hair. She stares out the window as the day begins to fade. Even though she is alone, her posture is perfect. Through the window, the fading city looks foreign to her and for a moment she can't recall where she is. To ride out the fear, she sits on the divan in her ivory silk sheath, spine straight, bare neck elongated, one foot slightly ahead of the other, as if she could rise at any moment.

The hotel suite is creamy and soft. In each room, the illumination is nature perfected. The woman glances at the glossy phone which is deliberately off the hook. She remembers pressing a pillow over the open-mouthed receiver until at last it ceased blaring. Still, the insistent red message light blinks. She ignores it and looks back out the window over the collection of rooftops, feels herself moving toward the edge of something decisive.

During this time, her daughter does not cross her mind.

*   *   *

Miranda walks the five blocks to the hotel. She feels dead inside, as if someone else were animating her body, forcing her forward along the sidewalk. She cannot feel her feet. The streets are darkening and lights begin to flicker along the avenue. The hotel facade is gleaming and illuminated with warm light, clean and inviting. The hotel is exclusive and luxurious. Its golden elevator had carried her upward on Sunday, which was only yesterday, she reminds herself. She remembers that she was starving; she had been rationing meals to save money, but her mother did not want to go down to the garden terrace for lunch, so they did not eat. Her beautiful mother looked thin, as if eating were not something she remembered to do these days. Instead, the two of them sat carefully at the glass dining table in her mother's suite, their hands folded in their laps, not quite looking at each other, their reflections lying flat on the glass surface. Her mother was living in the hotel for an undetermined time. A month ago, she had sold her penthouse and given away all of her things. "A transition," she explained, though it was no explanation at all. Her mother had only told her of this after all transactions had been completed. Miranda did not let on, but she was angry that her mother had given so much away when she herself was struggling.

At the glass table, they did not speak. Eventually, she realized her mother was staring at her neck, and she touched her fingers to her throat. Her pearls felt cool; they felt perfect and smooth. Their function was to lift Miranda to their ideal of cultivated dignity and self-assurance, but they did not always succeed.

Her mother rose silently, and as she moved away, her mother resembled a stranger, a slim ivory cipher. She disappeared into what must have been the bedroom, and returned with a necklace box, a china saucer, and a pair of small scissors, the type that came packaged in a hotel's sewing kit. Carefully, she laid the familiar blue velvet box on the table and unhooked the gold latch. Her manicured fingers turned the box so that Miranda could see the natural pearls inside. Miranda knew this necklace well. Her mother had worn it so often it had become a part of her. She was surprised she had not noticed it missing from her mother's neck.

"Give me your pearls."

Her mother's green eyes were neither demanding nor kind. Instead they had an unnerving empty quality. She clumsily unhooked her necklace and passed it over. For a fleeting moment, her mother laid a hand over hers; the hand was warm, and for some reason she was relieved to feel this. In the suite's perfect light, she could see that her pearls, while good quality, looked dull next to her mother's, which were astonishingly deep and luminous, tiny bluish globes close on a strand, keeping each other safe.

"I'm very thirsty," Miranda said. She got up quickly and went to the kitchenette. There was nothing in the refrigerator, and she did not want to ask her mother for the key to the minibar. Instead, she let the tap water run and filled a large glass and drank it rapidly. The water was cool as it slid down her throat and into her empty belly.

From the sink, she watched her mother situate the bone china saucer in front of her on the table. Her mother took up the scissors. Miranda suddenly felt hot. The water in her stomach surged. Something was off about her mother's mouth.

She heard a snip and a clink. She watched as her mother methodically slipped the sharp open blades between her cultured pearls, one by one, and snapped them shut. She leaned against the counter and closed her eyes; another pearl dropped into the saucer, and another. Each clink sounded loud inside her head. When the sound finally paused, she opened her eyes; silk cord lay in tatters on the glass.

She came back to the table. Her pearls sat quietly gathered in the saucer, huddled close. They looked sad and yellow against the blue-white bone china.

Her mother pointed to the saucer. Her voice was clear and insistent, but her eyes seemed hollow. "I don't believe you can see it. How dispiriting it is."

She opened her mouth to reply, though she didn't know what to say.

"Do you understand me?" Her mother's face strained.

Miranda nodded. She did not want to understand at all. She preferred to think about her paycheck lying in that saucer in useless pearly beads. She preferred to pretend those dead farmed pearls were the most urgent thing in the room.

With slender fingertips, her mother lifted one of Miranda's pearls from the china and brought it to her pale, dry lips. Miranda thought she might be preparing to kiss it. Instead, the pearl disappeared over her mother's tongue and she swallowed. Miranda stared at her.

After a few moments, her mother said, "Get me a glass of water, darling."

She did as she was told.

"Thank you." Her mother sipped at the glass before taking up another pearl.

Miranda could not bring her arm up to make it stop. Her mother seemed suddenly powerful. It was frightening. She watched her mother's determined green eyes, her delicate throat where the skin was beginning to slacken. One by one, she watched her cultured pearls disappear inside her mother's mouth. In the silence, she listened to her mother swallow.

When there was one pearl left, her mother spoke again: "You look worried, darling. Don't worry. I'm taking them with me."

There it was. A shaky panic overwhelmed her. She felt in the throes of a familiar emergency for which she was utterly ill prepared.

Her mother was calm. She closed the royal blue velvet box over the strand of luminous rare pearls and pushed it toward her. "For you," she said. "Everything else is gone. None of it would have been good for you anyway."

Miranda touched the box. The velvet felt pliant. The gold latch gleamed. Accepting it made her sick.

Her mother turned to look out the plate-glass window framed by thick ivory curtains. To Miranda, the skyline did not look real from inside this room. It had the gloss of an image of something that wanted to be real. "The finest pearl divers in Japan are women," her mother said. "It is a sisterhood. The job is very risky. It's dangerous to bring that kind of raw beauty up from below."

"I know." Her eyes felt hot. She felt something sharp probing the pit of her belly, depositing something false and hard.

Her mother's eyes looked sunken, clear green sunken pools. She stood. "I'm very tired." She moved to the divan and sat on its edge, and Miranda thought she looked too prim. Her mother leaned over to remove her shoes then swung her legs up and lay on her side. "Stay with me, darling. Until I fall asleep. Then I want you to leave."

She moved her chair next to her mother, and held her hand until she drifted off, eyelids twitching. Her free hand lifted to her mother's lips and felt for her breath.

*   *   *

Inside the hut, the women begin their rituals. After praying to Ishigami, they grease their bodies by the fire. They sing quietly and pass the can from one woman to the next. They help each other, rubbing grease over their sisters' strong backs. Afterward, the women sit in a circle and practice their breathing to prepare their lungs for the arduous work ahead. The ama can hold their breath longer than any human on earth. They can withstand the cold depths. During their dives, they surface into the contained pocket of air created by their overturned wooden bucket. When the ama breach, they let out a long piercing whistle—the *isobue*—that echoes like a plaintive siren over the water and through the fog, penetrating the early morning dreams of the fishermen and villagers on the verge of waking.

*   *   *

While her mother slept, she moved through the creamy hotel suite. She checked the bathroom and her mother's purse; she checked the empty closet and cabinets and drawers. The hotel windows, thankfully, did not open. The scissors on the glass table looked dangerous; she slipped them into her own coat pocket.

Ever since she was small, she had become expert at keeping her mother alive.

She wondered if she should call someone.

Standing at the window, the inside of her head felt heavy and blank. Outside, the world had grown black. She worried about going home so late on the subway. She argued with herself about staying. She imagined following her mother around the hotel suite like the child she no longer was, vigilant and trembling with terror and love, trying to block her mother from following through.

In her lowest moments, and there had been many, Miranda herself had considered the act. She had recognized its utility, its fatal pragmatism. This recognition had never failed to bring her calm. It felt decisive and honest. What right did she have to deny her mother this dignity by hounding her?

She dropped back into the chair next to the divan. The light was low and her mother seemed peaceful. Miranda rocked in her chair. She began to cry and could not stop. The crying infuriated her. She held onto her empty belly and rocked and struggled to convince herself that all would be well, because she was here and as long as she was here nothing could happen.

Her mother's eyes fluttered open, still half-asleep. She reached out her hand and her fingers brushed Miranda's arm then pushed. "Darling, please go away."

*   *   *

But here she is, the next evening, leaning into the cold wind, walking deliberately toward the hotel. She stops and again, for the umpteenth time, checks to make sure her cell phone is on. The hotel facade is sleek and glossy. At the entrance stands a different doorman. His uniform is thick and well cut. The long navy coat looks warm and elegant. His cheeks are red and he lifts his gloved hands to secure his hat against the wind. This is the doorman who, in a few hours, a little past midnight, will witness her mother's fall from the roof. After this night, he will not return to work at the hotel. But for now he is doing his job with genuine pleasure. Miranda stands to the side as he opens the door for a couple wrapped in black. From inside the hotel comes a warm rush of perfumed air. The sensation is alluring and she instinctively steps toward it; she wants to enter that warmth and fall asleep in its cushiony arms. She peers in through the glass at the vast lobby; the inside glows golden, like some kind of forever.

The doorman smiles broadly and holds the door open for her. "Miss?" She recognizes it is open just for her. The sweet air from inside warms her face.

"No. No, thank you." She lowers her head and steps quickly away, into the cold, her steps moving faster and faster until she is running up the avenue.

In her studio apartment she sits on the daybed with a single lamp on, still wearing her coat and scarf, overcome with shivering. Walking home, she desperately splurged on a bottle of cabernet she could not afford. She tries not to gulp the wine, forces her shaky hand to set down the glass after each drink.

The cell phone lies on the nightstand next to the bottle.

The confiscated scissors lie next to the phone.

Deep inside her mind, an alarm has been going off without ceasing. It has been jangling her whole life. In the quiet of her room, the alarm's escalating insistence is giving her a headache, like some distant emergency exit that should not be ajar but which she cannot locate to close.

Next to the scissors sits the necklace box she has given up trying to open. Unbidden, she wonders what Portia is doing in this moment. She wonders why the little girl's pale hair is so terribly thin. She wonders if Portia's mother is feeding her dinner. Then she realizes it is probably the nanny and she hopes the nanny is kind to her. She hopes Portia will forget the struggles of her day and find rest in sleep. The wine glass at her lips is empty again; she is sipping at air.

But when she reaches for the bottle, it topples, wavering at the table's edge, and she tries to grab with hands not fast enough, not steady enough. It falls toward the floor, an arc of cabernet splashing over the eyelet comforter, soaking into its white fibers. The bottle thuds to the hardwood and rolls like thunder, trailing dark liquid that pools and seeps in the hairline cracks between the planks. How can such a small thing undo you? The sobs come from somewhere so deep it is terrifying. For several long ragged breaths, they double her over. But they don't stop her from stripping off her winter scarf and dropping to her knees, trying hard to contain the mess that travels faster than she can catch, racing down the warp of the wood into the darkest corners she will never be able to reach.

* * *

On Hegura Island, the ama carry their oyster baskets and their wooden buckets to the end of the pier. Their bodies shine with grease, the stone pouches heavy around their necks. The waves are calm and lacy with foam this morning and the women are thankful. One after another, the ama breathe in; they fill their lungs with fresh air and dive, naked and brave, plunging into the cold water without a sound. Inside the sea, they are inverted and sleek; they pass down, down from the cold through warm currents, eyes open, their strong legs pushing them closer to the sleeping oyster beds, ever mindful of the shadowy creature that longs for them, the dark beast that lies in wait among the sharp rocks.

DAWNA KEMPER's fiction has appeared in Ecotone, ZYZZYVA, The Kenyon Review, Colorado Review, Shenandoah, Santa Monica Review, and elsewhere. She lives in Los Angeles, where she hosts and co-curates a quarterly reading series in Venice, CA.

June

V. Efua Prince

1

I dreamed I was carrying a dead man on my back. The stench of his decomposing flesh poisoned each breath. His weight bent my shoulders like a sack filled with cotton. He had been dead long enough for his flesh to yield its contents so I was soiled beneath the mass. But I held his arms and kept a labored pace. When I woke, I buried him without ceremony. I did not mark the date.

2

What's left? Memory. But where is it lodged? In the brain as images? In the flesh as disease or scar tissue? In the air like a virus? In the soil like seed? In the marrow of bone.

3

It was my baby, all grown up looking like herself but also a lot like me when I was her age. It was she that brought it all back.

No, she didn't do it.

All she did was stretch out and fill in. Legs long as a drag queen's with a switch full of conjure—drawing on her roots in New Orleans. I never let her spend a lot of time with her people down there. New Orleans is just too much. Music at all hours of the day and night. They eat anything that walk, swim, or crawl. They prone to painting their houses in audacious hues. Even the plants wear too many colors. In the yards, leaves lounge in every shade of green with some so bold they line their lips in red and powder on burgundy rouge. Lemon and orange trees sway beside palms. Air so thick down there that nothing bothers to mind. That's why they always dancing in the streets. A child ain't safe in that city. Nevertheless she's got that city in her roots.

Then too, her breasts grew way past any size I'm familiar with. Folks always looking at her saying, "Jill Scott." When she open her mouth they expect blue notes to slide out. She looking at them through big, luxurious eyes. Ethiopians walking up to her speaking Amharic and when she shakes her head at them they say, "Where you from?" She says, "Virginia." They say, "Oh. Where your people from?" "New Orleans," she says. "And Maryland." They look confused.

Those aren't places to be from.

4

I felt guilty. So when he called me and talked incessantly about whatever he was talking about I felt compelled to keep the line open. I didn't always listen. Sometimes I put the phone down and did other things. It really didn't matter since he never expected me to say anything. When I got back to the phone, he'd still be talking. He didn't seem to miss me. We had dated for nearly five years—my last years of high school and into college. By the time I broke up with him I was clear that our lives were on different paths. But I felt guilty for turning my attention to other men. For leaving whatever love I had for him on a shelf. He would call long distance and hold me on the phone for hours at a time, crying, yelling, accusing, pleading,

One morning he showed up at my house. I went to school in Virginia. I lived off-campus and nearly two hundred miles away from him but there he was. I let him in. My day hadn't started yet so I went to the bathroom and showered. I put on my underclothes, wrapped myself in a towel, and returned to my room where he was waiting. It's been too long now and I don't recall exactly how he approached me or why but he started tussling with me and tied my wrists up with one of his wifebeaters. Because I lived alone on the first floor of a house, I kept knives and scissors around in the event that a stranger would come into my abode entertaining the thought that I was a victim. In my room, I was never more than a few feet from some kind of sharp object. So when he pushed me onto my bed with my hands bound, I retrieved the blade I kept tucked between my box spring and bed frame and cut myself loose. He became enraged. "You cut my shirt!" Then he picked me up and carried me out into the hallway, opened the front door and threw me out onto the front porch, locking me out of my house. There I was—humiliated. In my bra and panties locked out of my own house in front of my neighbors and whoever happened by on our active street. I didn't dare make too much noise. I curled up as small as I could and I waited for release.

5

"It's always been a mystery to me how men can feel themselves honored by the humiliation of their fellow beings."
—*Mahatma Gandhi*

6

" . . . a group of touts attacked a woman at one of the major bus stations in the capital, Harare, [Zimbabwe] and stripped her naked for the 'crime' of wearing a miniskirt. She managed to escape after paying a commuter omnibus crew two dollars to hide her from the mob. Police arrested two of the attackers who are still in custody awaiting trial, but the other suspects are still at large."
—*Sally Nyakanyanga,* "Humiliation: The Latest Form of Gender Violence" in African Renewal, April 2015

7

Where you from?
Virginia.

8

In 1619 twenty Africans were offloaded at Old Point Comfort in the area which was to become Fort Monroe in Hampton, Virginia, about forty miles from the British settlement at Jamestown.

9

Sometimes I imagine a woman being coerced into sex with two or three men in public. She is initially reluctant but eventually gives herself over to the pleasure. The men have broken a trust to take advantage of her. These fantasies always figure white people; I think this is so that I am clear it isn't me. For years I would pray and ask God to heal my mind. I don't bother God with this any more. Now I think this is memory. I think it has something to do with things that happened when I was a very young child.

10

Virginia. New Orleans. Maryland.
Those aren't places to be from.

II

The boundaries of territory in its earliest formation were vaguely identified, particularly its western limits, and thus Virginia was conceived as extending from "sea to sea."

I2

When Europe began carving up the world to serve their royal houses, it justified its aggression using the machinations of binary thinking. Binary thinking conceives of experience in terms of oppositions—such as right or wrong, us or them, up or down— which one imagines as inherent rather than constructed by a society. This vision of the world as essentially oppositional is reflected in European religion that pictures divinity in terms of good and evil, light and darkness, heaven and hell. Europeans used this conceptual frame to impose order on their experiences. Human experience is chaotic enough with the confounding intrusions of everyday mysteries such as lightning strikes, wolves, the bubonic plague, famine, war, and about a million other things lurking in the shadows to suddenly kill you. But for Europeans living during the sixteenth, seventeenth, eighteenth, and nineteenth centuries the realm of possibility was undergoing dramatic expansion.

Technological developments were enabling previously unimaginable journeys across the seas. People were not only going across the water—some of them were coming back. It's no wonder then that Europeans insisted upon a framework that could readily impose order on these widely varied experiences. When the world was flat and the sun revolved around the Earth, things were far less confusing. Folks were saying, "There is nothing out there but death, which is not a problem because I have no need to go there; I am here at the center of all things." And so they found the notion of a round world orbiting the sun touted by that stargazing cleric Nicolaus Copernicus to be entirely perplexing. Copernicus suggested that perceiving aspects of reality required complex calculations that were beyond the average person's frame of reference derived from seeing, tasting, hearing, feeling, and smelling. They were being told that their raw senses could not be trusted (it certainly looks like the sun is circling the world). Copernicus and his erudite lot had science; those operating without the benefit of telescopes and mathematical equations needed *something* that could make sense of it all. Imagine the bewilderment propagated within poor societies by adventurers funded by venture capitalists seeking an untold cache of spices, sugar, and gold that they hoped to extract from exotic and distant lands. Even for those who stayed put, these new notions changed what people hoped for, how they saw themselves, and where they thought they were. But because their frame of reference tended to conceptualize in terms of the binary, these ocean journeys yielded for Europeans a "New World" rather than an expanded worldview.

In fact, the conceptual framework fostered by binary thinking encourages a kind of cognitive dissonance. Human beings make analogical comparisons in order to encode something not yet experienced. We come to understand the new thing by mapping it onto something familiar. In this way conceptual maps are merely a long series of associations between dissimilar things. The comparison, then, between what the Europeans knew and what they were freshly encountering is quite natural. However, the trouble comes with the insistence that these encounters be mapped in terms of binary oppositions. Binary thinking represented the lands on the other side of the Atlantic as a *world* somehow distinct, somewhere separate and apart from the world Europeans had already known. Rather than a "New World" and an "Old World," there is, for all practical purposes, just one world. Thus, in terms of a concept, "New World" is a bad metaphor that fails to reconcile with basic reality. Still, the idea of it fit for a people who were more concerned with liberating themselves from European constraints than they were with taking the time to consider the implications of their metaphors.

13

Virginia is a metaphor for the New World.

14

"On the thirty-third day after leaving Cadiz I came into the Indian Sea, where I discovered many islands inhabited by numerous people. I took possession of all of them for our most fortunate King by making public proclamation and unfurling his standard, no one making any resistance."
—*Christopher Columbus*, 1493

15

When we think of rape we are encouraged to envision it as a problem between individuals. The reality, however, is much more pernicious. Rape is an ideology. It is a way of thinking about the world and its inhabitants that only belatedly manifests as sexual assault.

16

Knock knock
Who's there?
Me
Me who?
Let me in my house motherfucker

17

According to Michael Doran in his *Atlas of County Boundary Changes in Virginia 1634-1895,* "Either as an Anglicized modification of a local chieftain's name (Win-gi-na) or in unabashed flattery of the distaff English sovereign, [Sir Walter] Raleigh's lands became known as Virginia."

18

Virginia. Virgin land. No one lives there. A wilderness peopled not but by savages.

19

Knock knock
Who's there?
No one
No one who?
Noonenoonenoonenoone

20

More than 350 years ago, Captain John Smith might have walked the ground beneath the porch I crouched on. The great captain might have paused on this patch of earth to finger the charter for the Virginia Company given him by the sovereign King James. He might have offered a trifle in exchange for a smile from an Indian child right on this ground. Captain Smith might have had corn grown on this very patch of earth. He might have rested on a log right here on his way to visit Chief Powhatan. He might have squatted here too, to take aim at an Indian warrior shooting buckshot in defense of his land. He might have taken aim to piss. This might very well have been the actual spot where John Smith himself carved a hole in the dirt wherein he relieved his bowels.

I should erect a monument.

21

There are no heroes.
Villains neither.

22

People do not talk about the horrendous conditions in Europe as
an explanation for European colonialism and imperialism. Instead,
American school children are shown pictures of pilgrims seeking
religious freedoms. One of the best known of these early settlers
is John Winthrop whose vision of founding a "city upon the hill"
is indicative of a kind of binary thinking. The pilgrim story of a
people fleeing religious persecution, intent on building a model
society, casts the travelers in the light of a hero. Winthrop draws
this image from Matthew 5:14–16 in the New Testament of the
Bible which states, "You are the light of the world. A town built
on a hill cannot be hidden. Neither do people light a lamp and
put it under a bowl. Instead they put it on its stand, and it gives
light to everyone in the house. In the same way, let your light shine
before others, that they may see your good deeds and glorify your
Father in heaven." By representing their actions in the language
of this sacred text, Winthrop associates their actions with that of
Jesus Christ—the ultimate Western hero. On the other side of this
narrative is the villain.

23

While the pilgrims ultimately settle the Massachusetts Bay Colony, Winthrop set out in 1620 with a charter for Virginia.

24

"Rape is not the problem. Rape is a symptom of the problem. And the answer is not to attempt to stop men from raping women, but to categorically change women's values and status in their communities."

—*Abigail Disney* cited in Merger 2012

25

The Chinese still grieve over Japanese aggressions during the early parts of World War II, which resulted in what is known as the Rape of Nanjing. Estimates range widely but official records state that two hundred thousand Chinese were massacred and some twenty to thirty thousand were raped during the Japanese campaign beginning in December 1937. In *Nanjing Requiem,* Chinese American novelist Ha Jin writes about the heroic efforts of an American missionary, Minnie Vautrin, to spare as many young women as she can from the horrors of the Japanese occupation. Western readers love heroes. Creating heroes provides a way to elevate an individual out of her social, cultural, and historical circumstances. It alleviates responsibility for collective action, so long as we can look to heroic action for change. But rape is not really about individuals, especially during times of war. After killing those whom one intends to kill, what is a more effective strategy for dominating a resistant people than rape? Raping a woman—girl, baby, grandmother, great-grandmother—in front of her family and friends is extremely effective at unraveling the fabric of the community. The sense of shame born by the women and the sense of failure born by the men undermine the foundational security needed to stabilize a community. Rape erodes trust. It is psychologically devastating, not to mention the myriad concerns to one's health and physical well-being. And what of the children born of rape? Who will love them and more importantly *how* will they love them—it's not a question of *if* someone will love because the human capacity to love is tremendous. But *how* one loves is another question. What kind of love results in the aftermath of rape?

26

Funny thing: I don't remember how I got off the porch.

27

How one loves in the aftermath of rape is a question that African Americans are still resolving. In the wake of slavery, we have demonstrated the extended capacity to envision the rape of black women at the hands of white men, partly because it reinforces the illusion of white, male power as well as the desirability of black women. More recently, African American women authors like Alice Walker and Ntozake Shange popularized (a terrible characterization but I think accurate) the image of black women victimized at the hands of black men. However, if we are more honest and begin to explore the dynamics of rape and the culture it breeds then we might see more clearly the men who are not just perpetrators but those who are victims as well. For instance, while rape is largely perpetuated against women, the notion that it is exclusively violent men acting against women is preposterous. Do we have any idea how many men were raped under slavery? When we divest from gender politics enough to explore the dynamics at work, then we might begin to reflect on rape as a kind of disease, rather like rabies, a mortal contagion corrupting the DNA of a society. Then we can explore the ways it appears as a symptom of a pandemic degrading the host as well as its victim.

It's been years since the United Nations Security Council declared rape a war crime, unanimously adopting Resolution 1820, which called for the immediate and complete halt to acts of sexual violence in 2008. Yet on July 6, 2014, the *Guardian* published the article, "Turning a Blind Eye to Rape Crimes in the Democratic Republic of the Congo," accusing the prime minister, Augustin Matata Ponyo, of refusing to acknowledge that state security services outside of the conflict region, including the capital of Kinshasa, are using rape as torture. Rape is such an effective means of subduing a people precisely because of the inclination to turn a blind eye. No one wants to see, let alone watch, an act so heinous that it threatens to corrode the very foundation of civilization. Rape has the potential to leave its victims incapacitated and unable to raise a family—there is no more devastating impact of war.

Outside the boundaries of war, rape is more circumspect. The subject of rape as a military tactic remains taboo and the United States has been adopting measures to curb sexual assaults within the ranks of its own military. On another front, in April 2014, the White House appointed a task force to curb sexual assaults on college campuses. Rape is all over the news these days. According to a survey reported by the Associated Press on July 9, 2014, two in five (that's 40 percent) of colleges/universities have not investigated a single rape in the previous five years. Nevertheless, the

White House estimates that one in five women (that's 20 percent) graduate as victims of sexual assault. And if one in five women, how many young men? And how many are graduating as rapists? Rape should not be built in to the cost of education.

28

Funny thing: In 1421, when Admiral Zheng's Ming fleet reached the Western Hemisphere from China he did not find Virginia. He wasn't looking for a New World—and so he did not find one. He encountered land—fecund—but not vacant. Desirable—but not prone.

V. EFUA PRINCE is the author of Burnin' Down the House, Daughter's Exchange, and numerous essays including "Empty Vessel," "Amita," and "On Metaphor." She is an Associate Professor of African American Studies at Wayne State University and has served as an Associate Professor of English and Black Studies and as director of Black Studies at Allegheny College, the Avalon Professor of Humanities at Hampton University, a visiting scholar at the University of Virginia's Carter G. Woodson Institute, and a fellow at Harvard University's W. E. B. Du Bois Institute. Prince received her PhD from the University of Michigan in English Language and Literature.

Paper Boats

Lydia Martín

The *quimbombó* had a stink to it that Felipe Mirabal couldn't pinpoint. He walked into the cooler to sniff what remained of the ground pork the cook had used. But the pork was virtuous. And Felipe had received the okra himself early that morning—two crates full of fuzzy, bright green pods that snapped cleanly in half with the slightest pressure of his thumb.

"Okra on the stove always smells a little manly. Like—well, you know like what," said Rufino the cook, and the other guys guffawed.

"Álvaro, grab that pot!" Felipe threw elbow-length mitts to the brawniest guy in the kitchen, a Cuban rafter who had paddled strung-together inner tubes onto a rocky beach in the Upper Keys a year earlier.

The paddle Álvaro wielded now came from a kitchen supply store and was for flipping long strips of pork-back frying in a tank of lard that perpetually brimmed over, a thin layer of the stuff always congealing underfoot, making Álvaro's workstation as treacherous as an ice rink. But those crunchy, salty chicharrones, sold from the walk-up window in brown paper bags that quickly turned translucent from the grease, remained the runaway hit at Restaurante La Rampa, at the southern tip of Miami Beach.

"Take it to the dumpster! *Sí, sí*—pot and all!" Felipe, his silver hair in a pompadour, a black comb always tucked into the breast pocket of his impeccable white shirts, threw himself against the back door and held it open.

He had run a scrupulous kitchen from day one. But lately, no matter how he tried to stay on top of things, there seemed to be more and more ugly little surprises. He was starting to think someone wanted to sabotage his business. It had to be someone right under his nose. Last week, he had been forced to pour ten gallons of milk down the drain. Someone playing games had unplugged the front cooler the night before.

And there was the incident a week before *that,* which Felipe still couldn't get out of his head. He was about to bite into a steak sandwich, his tie thrown over his shoulder, when a rat the size of a well-fed kitten scampered across the lunch counter. Only Felipe and the waiter who had brought his sandwich saw it.

In the early 1990s, the southernmost streets of South Beach hadn't yet caught the renaissance fever flaring a few blocks to the north, where decrepit Art Deco hotels were getting splashed in fresh pastels and out-of-towners were snatching boarded-up buildings like they were dollar-store souvenirs. The famous fashion photographers and the packs of models were constantly descending, elbowing one another for sexy backdrop. If you could call the subtropical decay they chased *sexy.*

And now there was talk of luxury condo towers going up near La Rampa. The restaurant's tiny south-of-Fifth enclave, hugged by the ocean on one side and the bay on the other, and lapped at its tip by the wake of cruise ships crossing Government Cut channel, had grown seedier and seedier since the Beach's last heyday back in the 1960s. Once the sun went down, you knew better than to be on foot there.

The restaurant still drew crowds, thank God. La Rampa and Joe's Stone Crab down the street were about the only life left in Miami Beach's oldest subdivision. But Felipe knew there'd be no stopping developers who were already sewing together parcels of land. The four squat apartment buildings across the street and the bodega next to it had already been knocked down, their flattened lots sending up garbage and grit whenever a big enough breeze blew off the Atlantic. City officials hadn't yet approved the idea of high-rises cluttering Felipe's piece of sky. But Miami Beach was suddenly drunk on its own promise—of course they'd vote to let the developers build as high as they pleased. That's why Felipe was pretty sure someone wanted his restaurant to fail, so he would be forced to sell for cheap. His parking lot alone took up more than half an acre.

* * *

"There are just too many strange things happening," he told his son, Luisito, who was driving them to see another rundown house for sale in mainland Miami. "Today with the quimbombó—how could it have spoiled like that? And what about that rat a couple of weeks ago? I've seen a lot of greasy kitchen rats in my time. That was no kitchen rat!"

"What are you saying, Papi? A rat is a rat."

"No, mijito. That rat looked like somebody's pet! I'm telling you, somebody wants to ruin me."

"You mean you think someone planted the rat? Por favor, Papi! Where do you get these things?"

Luisito was fresh from his evening workout, his salon-sculpted hair still damp and the V-neck of his designer t-shirt too plunging for his father's taste, he knew. He downshifted and punched the accelerator to make the light at Biscayne Boulevard and Thirty-Sixth Street. They shot north, past hookers, crackheads, slummy motels with crisp midcentury modern lines.

"Two Ivy League degrees and what do you understand about life? *Espabila, mijo!* Wake up already! And why are you taking me to see another shitty house in the same bad neighborhood?" Felipe had promised to give Luisito a down payment for the right investment, but the three houses he had seen so far were nothing but dumps.

Felipe and his son had been close once. When Luisito was a boy, he'd settle into the crook of Felipe's arm to watch TV while his mother Rosalina baked flans for the restaurant, flooding the house with the warm scent of caramel and vanilla. When he was about to turn twelve, Felipe inched away. "You're almost a man already," he had said. "Grown men don't cuddle."

There were lots of things grown men didn't do, and Felipe suddenly wanted to make sure Luisito understood the rules. Grown men didn't cry, of course. But grown men also didn't go to the mall with their mothers to pick out towel sets. They didn't sit with their legs delicately crossed at the ankles. They left their eyebrows bushy, even when the women in the family produced tweezers.

Luisito had been back from school two years now—Brown for undergrad, Cornell for a master's in architecture—and even though father and son lived in the same area code again, they were only drifting farther apart. They checked in by phone every few days, but they seldom managed to get together. When they did, there wasn't much to discuss. It was too hot. The price of gas had gone up again. Yes, Luisito's work at the big firm was going well. Yes, Felipe still played dominoes with his old buddies from the University of Havana.

But Luisito had no real sense anymore of how Felipe filled his hours away from the restaurant. And Felipe didn't dare ask too many questions of Luisito. It didn't help that Luisito couldn't stomach Felipe's hard-line on everything to do with Cuban politics. They had gone at it time and time again. "How did I raise a socialist right under my own roof?" Felipe had yelled more than once. "How are you my son?"

A few weeks ago, Luisito had gone to see a famous jazz pianist from Havana who had headlined many times in Manhattan but was risking a Miami show for the first time. A mob of white-haired protesters waved Cuban flags, while a younger, courser crowd hurled obscenities and fists at ticketholders filing into the theater past bomb-sniffing dogs. Luisito regretted that he'd never be able to tell his dad about that night. Felipe might have been proud of him for sitting there with his stomach clenched against the urge to sob, feeling deeply Cuban as the hated communist pounded out a surreal "El Manisero" followed by a Havana-infused version of "Autumn Leaves," which happened to be his mother's favorite.

They got to the latest fixer-upper, a two-story Spanish Mediterranean on a generous lot, before the realtor arrived. Felipe went around the back and pushed open a swollen kitchen door. Most of the arched windows were busted and the vaulted ceiling in the dining room was starting to cave in.

But, oh, the cobalt tilework, the flamingo frieze above the Deco limestone fireplace, the courtyard littered with blood-red hibiscus flowers. Carried away by the potential of this new find, Luisito make a stupid confession: "Last weekend I went to an opening at the Valls Gallery and I bought an amazing photograph, really huge, that would be perfect above this fireplace!" The artist, who still lived in Cuba, captured a lacy refraction of light across the bluest swimming pool, in which he had floated giant white paper boats, all of them imprisoned by their concrete borders.

"You mean that place that sells overpriced art by a bunch of *maricones* with their noses up Fidel's ass?" Felipe pulled a cologne-doused handkerchief from his back pocket and pressed it to his temple, though a cool bay breeze played through the empty house. "That's what you do with your money? You give it to the regime?"

"It *is* my money, Papi. So all of their art is worthless because they happen to live on the island? I don't know why I keep trying to talk sense to a dinosaur!"

"*Your* money? Maybe you should be counting on *your* money and not mine to buy the house you want. How much did you pay for *esa mierda*?" Felipe walked out the front door, but at the landing, he stopped to pry off a piece of the crumbling keystone, encrusted with swirls of ancient sea life. Coquina, it was called in Cuba. His favorite beaches in Matanzas, the ones the tourists never visited, were filled with it. He held a rough shard in his palm, put it in his pocket, then pulled it out and flung it, smacking the trunk of a coconut palm that had grown horizontally across the front lawn.

He stepped back inside. "I'm a dinosaur? And what are you? Artists on the island paint only what Fidel lets them paint. The ones with the timbales to say what they want to say are still being persecuted and jailed, and here it is 1992. You see brave commentary in that photo you bought? It's all calculated commentary, to help that *hijo de puta* seem more open these days. So that they can sell art to idiots like you who support the very bastards who destroyed your homeland."

"I was born at Mount Sinai Hospital up the street, remember? And I'd rather extend a hand to the younger generation in Cuba, because after all, Castro is not their fault! And that bile is going to kill you!"

Rosalina had died in the same hospital a decade earlier. The cancer spread quickly, turning her into a shrunken *viejita* virtually overnight. But in her last days, she had spoken with a force and clarity that seemed otherworldly.

"Luisito, *mi niño*, you're going to live your life however you want. I've always accepted you. But your father, he never will. Don't break his heart. Get married and have a family the way God intended. Nobody has to know what you do on the side."

The morning after the quimbombó incident, Felipe was eyeing the newest guy, who was mashing mounds of garlic for sofrito, when a solemn-faced waitress came to the kitchen. "I'm sorry to bother you, Don Felipe. But there are people here for you."

In the dining room, one of the visitors was holding a wet rag to his nose. La Rampa always passed inspection, but this time, two men from the state took notes while they popped lids off storage containers, poked their heads into refrigerators and freezers and stuck thermometers into cooked hams and marinating chickens. By the time it was all over, the inspectors had uncovered seventeen violations, from mold in the ice maker to fetid rags being used by wait staff to meat kept in coolers nine degrees too warm.

Luisito's pager buzzed itself off a nightstand and fell apart on the marble floor of his rented Mid-Beach apartment. He was searching for the battery under the bed when the landline started ringing.

"I've been calling for fifteen minutes!"

"*Qué pasa*, Papi?"

"I told you somebody wanted to ruin me! Didn't I tell you? And some *maricón* must have called the media. There are four news trucks outside. They're interviewing people at the takeout window!"

* * *

In the early 1960s, when Felipe was an assistant professor of marine biology at the University of Havana, the new Castro government began its campaign to purge the faculty of any *elemento contrarevolucionario.* He spent three years in a rural prison for subversion, for grumbling to colleagues about the other professors who were being arrested for nothing. He chopped sugarcane by day and chewed it by night to take the edge off his hunger. There was no trial, no sentence. He wasn't sure he'd ever get out, but in case he ever did, he started learning English from the professor of philology who shared his cell. *Cerca,* "near." *Lejos,* "far." *Cuando,* "when?" *Pronto,* "soon." They also shared a safety pin to pop the blisters that formed on their scholars' hands after those endless hours of forced labor in the fields.

Felipe and Rosalina arrived in Miami in 1965 and slept on the floor of a studio apartment belonging to cousins of hers who worked as bellboys at side-by-side hotels on Collins Avenue. Three days after landing, Felipe strolled into Suwannee's Seafood House and made an impression on the owners, bearded brothers from backwater Florida who had moved down to *Miamah* in the 1940s. Felipe's English was "as good as them refugee Cuban bankers down on Eighth Street," the brothers figured out quickly.

After three weeks as a busboy, they promoted him to oyster shucker. Two weeks after that, he was a waiter in burgundy vest and matching bow tie. It was much cleaner work, but when he got to their first tiny apartment at one or two in the morning, his pockets stuffed with ones and fives, he still had to throw his clothes in a bucket of water and borax that Rosalina left for him in at the kitchen's threshold. She was pregnant with Luisito, and even the faintest whiff of fish turned her stomach. Felipe would plunge his uniform, his underwear, and his socks into the bucket—and then, before showering, he'd stand naked at the kitchen sink, rubbing a mixture of lemon juice and sugar into his hands like a surgeon.

One morning, before Felipe punched in at work, the brothers sat him down to tell him they were planning on moving back north to set up a fishing camp near the mouth of the Suwannee River.

"Miamah's gettin' outta hand," one of the brothers said.

"What about this place?" Felipe was already running through a mental list of other decent restaurants that might hire him.

"That's the good news, son," the other brother said. "We're gonna lease it to *you!* A little later, maybe we'll even let you buy us out. The Beach could use a good Cuban restaurant. Why should the mainland have them all? You got the smarts. And that wife of yours sure can cook. You just find five grand for a down payment and it's yours."

Felipe had a little money tucked away, but nothing close to that. "Look, you want to get back home. Believe me, I understand. I can give you one thousand dollars upfront, and send you a hundred a month, with interest, until I've paid off the rest."

Felipe changed the name to Restaurante La Rampa, a reference to a section of Calle 23, the main street through Havana's Vedado neighborhood. He and Rosalina moved there, just a few blocks from the university, soon after they were married. On Sunday mornings, when life seemed already so settled, they'd stroll the bustling La Rampa down to the sea, holding hands and fantasizing about their next apartment, which would have higher ceilings and a water view.

Restaurante La Rampa served fish every day like Suwannee's had, but it was most popular on Fridays, when the Catholic clientele demanded it. After Rosalina gave birth, she'd come in to direct the boiling of grouper heads for silky, golden soup, and the frying of whole red snappers fragrant with garlic and cumin. She also taught the kitchen staff to cook roasted pork that could melt in your mouth, black bean soup thick like chocolate batter, *arroz con pollo* creamy as risotto. Soon the place was so busy Felipe had to hire a girl just to handle the line at the door. By the time Luisito was seven, the Mirabals had made enough money to buy a boxy but roomy house at the edge of the Alton Road golf course, a towering Royal Poinciana ablaze in red blooms on the front lawn and the two mango trees out back heavy with fruit.

* * *

Luisito pulled up to the house, which seemed to have gotten a fresh coat of white since he last visited, to drive his father to the cardiologist. His blood pressure had been dangerously high since a couple days earlier, when the inspectors showed up. Luisito found Felipe out front, gazing up at the poinciana though it was too early in the summer for blooms.

"There's something I want to say." Felipe groaned as he dropped into the passenger seat of Luisito's roadster. They were finally leaving Mount Sinai, where the cardiologist, an old buddy of Felipe's from school, increased the dosage of his hypertension meds and instructed him to take a few days off from work—starting immediately.

"Just listen for a second before you start with your attacks," Felipe said. "Let's say there's no developer trying to get my restaurant to fail."

"OK. Let's say that."

"What if I've been infiltrated by spies instead? I can't sleep since I started turning this over. I should fire the new guy, the one who claims he escaped Cuba on a Jet Ski that he stole from the resort where he worked. Don't you think there would have been something in the paper? Remember those two Cubans who windsurfed here? They were in the news for days."

"Wait, wait. Spies from Cuba? Are you crazy?" But Luisito didn't have it in him for one of his usual tirades. He was suddenly feeling a tinge sick. Maybe Felipe *was* acting a little—well, not exactly crazy. But, spies? Could his father be showing signs of dementia? How old was he now, seventy-three?

"Why not spies from Cuba?" Felipe raised the passenger window against the wind whipping through the open convertible. "They're crawling all over Miami. That's been more than proven! They're sent here to gather information and wreak havoc. They probably know I give a lot money to anti-Castro groups. They have to have a file on me still, from the prison days. They keep track of their enemies."

Luisito was caught off guard when his eyes misted over, but he looked away before Felipe noticed. His father's generation was still so traumatized. Three decades into exile, they were still unwilling to leave the past in the past. His father was going to stoke his pain until the end, and take it with him to the grave. Just like his mother had done.

And Lord knows that whole generation was paranoid. After all, it was a Cuban exile fleeing Castro, Luisito had discovered a few years back, who had come up with the classic *Spy vs. Spy* cartoon. He still had a stack of the *Mad* magazines in which they appeared, magazines he had cherished even before knew there was anything Cuban about them.

"I never bothered to tell you about the castor oil," Felipe said. "I found a liter of it in the storage room. It was hidden behind the big cans of tomato sauce. Now, you tell me—what was that doing in my kitchen? If that gets poured into the food, my customers would have the shits for days. That's probably what was in the quimbombó."

"I'm going to try to look into all of it, Papi. But promise you'll stay home for a few days and rest, like the doctor said."

Luisito asked for time off from the firm where he was helping draw plans for a chain of resorts angling to blanket the Caribbean. He arrived at the restaurant the morning after the cardiologist appointment with a fruit smoothie in one hand and his father's briefcase in the other. He hadn't spent much time at La Rampa lately. He was a vegetarian now and his "neurotic diet" was one more disappointment to his father, who would look at him in disgust when he rejected La Rampa's celebrated *boliche* roast, orange grease dribbling from its chorizo-impaled center.

The sweet smells of espresso brewing, milk scorching, and buttered Cuban bread toasting in the sandwich presses for breakfast reminded Luisito of his childhood, when he'd go table to table doodling on regulars' paper placemats. He had to turn them over for white space; their fronts were crowded with illustrations of historic Cuban landmarks. When he got sleepy, he'd crawl under the skirted silverware table for naps, pretending he was a soldier bunking down in a fort.

Now he walked into the kitchen with the official list of violations in his hand, as the cook was taking delivery of onions, plantains, potatoes, some kind of greens.

"Do you want to inspect this stuff?" Rufino looked glad that Luisito had finally shown up.

"No, Rufi, you do it. I don't know what a good potato looks like." Felipe didn't believe in delegating and had never entertained the idea of hiring a manager. Maybe now was the time to find someone, or move Rufi into the job. But how would he convince his father?

The chicharrón guy was hefting a giant pan of pork rinds that had just come out of his fryer. It was that juicy meat attached to the crisped layer of skin that made La Rampa's chicharrones the most sought after in town. Luisito watched him scatter fistfuls of salt over them, his veins running like purple ropes down his arms. The man grabbed tongs to offer him one of the golden-brown rinds, and Luisito realized he'd stared a beat too long.

"How's your father?" the chicharrón guy asked.

"Worried." Luisito was careful not to make eye contact. "I'll be in the office if anyone needs me."

The violations seemed easy enough to correct. Luisito started by ordering a new ice maker and two boxes of kitchen linens. The coolers had just needed maintenance. When the repairman came that very morning and started swapping out compressor relays and condenser coils, Rufino, who had been in charge of the cooking for more than a dozen years, leaned in to watch.

"I told your father a long time ago that he needed to call somebody to fix the refrigerators," he said. "One night he decided he was going to fix the one out front himself. In the end all he did was wipe the dusty coils with a rag. And he must have forgotten to plug it back in. The next morning he was looking for someone to blame. *El pobre*. He's getting old, you know."

A guy from the kitchen supply showed up with new towels.

"There's already several boxes of them in the storage room," one of the waiters told Luisito. "Your father seemed to be stockpiling them, but he never let us open them. I'm not sure what he was waiting for."

The last time Luisito remembered being at the restaurant, the man was climbing bar stools to change light bulbs and hauling fifty-pound sacks of rice with no problem. Luisito hadn't been paying enough attention. A few weeks back they'd gone to eat at Felipe's favorite Chinese restaurant, and he'd hardly touched his shrimp-fried rice. The same thing had happened at the diner where they sometimes met on Sunday mornings. Felipe ordered his usual French toast and bacon, but left most on his plate.

It was nearly two in the morning when Luisito left the restaurant, exhausted from reading over time sheets and paying vendors and trying to figure out a better system for dating perishables—one of the tougher violations to fix. He knew he smelled like onions and grease, but he walked over to Maelstrom anyway.

As usual, there was a crowd of older men sitting at the tables out front, where you could have a conversation without having to scream over the pounding house music inside the club, the domain of buff boys in cutoffs and Doc Martens. Luisito rarely hung out in the patio, afraid his father might drive by one night and spot him with all of those maricones. But it was late enough, and the last thing he needed was to strobe out on the dance floor with a mob of shirtless guys high on Special K. What he needed was a cold beer.

"*Oye*, jefe!"

Luisito turned to see the chicharrón guy leaning against an olive tree aglow with tiny lights. He wore stiff Levis and a black button-down that showed a hint of chest hair at the collar. Body hair was becoming a strange sight on South Beach, where all the boys pumped iron and waxed, and looked like legions of smooth Roman statues.

"Álvaro Roque," the man said and extended a hand. "Do you know that in Havana, La Rampa is the street where all the gay people hang out?"

"That probably wasn't true when my parents were still in Cuba." Luisito looked around for a server. Now the whole restaurant would confirm he was gay. He didn't give a damn about the staff knowing, but he needed to protect his father from another blow right now.

"Did you find your spy yet?" Álvaro swallowed the rest of his Heineken. "Don't worry, your father tells me everything. I go over to the house sometimes and help him with the yard for a little extra cash."

"Maybe *you're* the spy. What do you know about castor oil?" Luisito tried to take on Álvaro's teasing tone, but he was suddenly self-conscious about his clumsy Spanish. Álvaro was one of those Cubans who spoke unhurried, luxurious Spanish, pronouncing every consonant.

"I know it'll give you diarrhea," Álvaro said. "The sandwich guy, *el nicaraguense,* gave a big bottle of it to your papi a few weeks ago when he was complaining that he had been stopped up for days. You know Cubans don't get enough fiber. Your dad never drinks water, either. But I've been trying to change his ways."

"And my dad listens to you?"

"I was a doctor in Cuba. But who wasn't? You should spend a little time with your *viejo,* you know. He's lonely. And, look, forgive me for saying this—maybe you stay away because you don't want him to know the details of your life. But he already knows."

"My father told you I'm gay? Does he know *you're* gay?" Luisito needed that beer.

"He told me he prays one day you'll find a quality *person* to be with." Álvaro motioned to a server. "And, yes, he knows I'm gay because the first time I went over to help him with the yard, I let drop about my ex-boyfriend the orchid specialist."

Luisito bought Álvaro another Heineken. And then another. They talked about the trellis Álvaro was helping his father build so they'd have room to hang all the orchids he was growing these days. And about Álvaro's horrific three days at sea, about the buddies who had pushed off from Cuba with him on a moonless night and disappeared a few hours later, unable to hang on when twelve-foot waves started knocking their raft around.

But Álvaro insisted he didn't want to dwell on the ugly stuff, so instead he talked about whitewashing the house, while Felipe stirred pails and brought iced water and shots of espresso, and later his homemade fried chicken and macaroni salad, which they ate on a blanket Felipe stretched out on the lawn. Luisito was wide-eyed at all of it. His father growing orchids? Making picnics? Whenever he would get stuck, unable to find the word he wanted in Spanish, he'd say it in English, and Álvaro managed to guess what he meant.

"I have an idea," Álvaro said. "How about you teach me some English and I'll teach you some Spanish? And there's probably other stuff we can teach each other. For example, I happen to know a few things about tending to rare orchids."

When Maelstrom closed at five in the morning, the last of the boys pairing up and stumbling off, Luisito and Álvaro walked down to the pier to watch the sun rise over the Atlantic. *Pier,* "muelle." *Olas,* "waves." *Una cita,* "a date."

They parted on the sidewalk in front of La Rampa. Álvaro had chicharrones to fry. But later that morning, they'd agreed, Luisito would join him and Felipe on a trip the two had planned to a farm in Homestead that grew the craziest orchids of all.

Luisito turned to leave, but then turned back. "Wait, what about the quimbombó?"

"That will go down as one of the great mysteries. I had a bowl of it before your father decided it was bad. It smelled like regular quimbombó to me."

The phone woke Felipe, who had spent another night on the sofa. He was still in his trousers, the TV replaying the highlights of a soccer match. Luisito was on the line saying he was going to join him and Álvaro in Homestead today. How the hell had that come to be?

"Maybe we'll get lunch after the orchids at this great little Mexican place down there," Luisito said. "Or, no! We can go for ribs at that barbecue shack near the Everglades. You remember how much you and mom loved the Miccosukee fry bread they make?"

Luisito sounded buoyant, like there was no trouble at all at La Rampa, like there wasn't at least a giant public-relations nightmare to fix after the violations and the news reports. But something about his son's tone, so light and so rare, plus the promise of a day with him and Álvaro both, had suddenly lifted Felipe's spirits, too.

He padded into the kitchen in bare feet to make his *café con leche*. It had been days since he had seen his slippers. He had searched all of the bedrooms, all of the bathrooms. When they'd bought this house, he and Rosalina had planned on more babies to fill it. They stopped trying after three miscarriages. "Luisito will have a family of his own someday and they'll use this house the way it was intended," Felipe said whenever Rosalina suggested they downsize.

She'd groused about all the upkeep but refused to hire even a part-time housekeeper, saying she didn't want another woman running her house. Felipe came to understand, much too late, that Rosalina kept a sparkling house as a form of self-flagellation. She was always leaving the scent of lavender in her wake as she towel-mopped the five bedrooms, the formal living room and dining room no one set foot in, and the few rooms they did use—as if the place had been regularly trampled by a ghost version of the big family she couldn't give him.

After her death, Felipe had hired a series of cleaning women who didn't clean well enough or meddled too much. The current one came once a week—just to hide his things. He couldn't keep track of his keys anymore. Or the mail he was certain he'd set down in one place and would appear days later in another.

Rosalina was already gone when Luisito went off to college, and it was only then that Felipe considered selling the house. "It suddenly feels like an isolation chamber. I may start talking to the walls soon," he told his son during one of their weekly phone chats, and he immediately wished he could take it back. He was proud of his *chamaquito*, who took after his papi at least when it came to scholarship. Luisito didn't deserve being guilted for chasing his dreams.

Truth was, Felipe knew he'd stay in this house until the end. There was nothing more disorienting than losing your sacred ground, the objects that reverberated with your own history. He had already lost everything once: an entire island, all of his beaches, most of his people. If he sold this house, gone forever would be Rosalina's sewing room, the Singer that she'd left threaded, her collection of shears still hanging from the pegboard. What would he do with the photographs on the walls, the china cabinet full of delicate things that only came out when Rosalina needed to fill the house with the sound of a crowd, usually selections of old friends from back home, all of them still adrift one way or another, even after so many years in Miami.

Every house on the mainland that Luisito had taken Felipe to see also was way too big for a man without a family. But if his son wanted to throw himself into restoring that last one, *qué carajo*, he wouldn't stand in the way. Everything he owned would go to Luisito one day anyhow. Maybe they could redo that crumbled coquina at the front landing themselves. Felipe still remembered enough from his marine-biology days to fill that dried-out pond out back with koi, and keep the water balanced. They could pay Álvaro to help with the work.

He had such an easy rapport with Álvaro. Why not with his own son? He and Álvaro could talk about almost anything while they were bent over the orchids, carefully inserting a single pollen grain from one plant into the slit of another. The first time Alvaro had come over, it was because Felipe had needed an extra pair of hands to help build a toolshed to replace the one that had rusted out. Felipe figured the muscle-bound chicharrón guy, who had just arrived from Cuba, would be grateful for the chance to make a little extra money. Behind the old shed they found a graveyard of orchids in pots, most of them just dry sticks, some miraculously flowering even though Rosalina, who preferred them to cut flowers, had banished them from the house and forgotten about them as soon as they lost their blooms.

"Orchids are naughty," Álvaro had said. "Not only can they be bisexual, not only can they trick male insects into having sex with them, but they can have reproductive sex with themselves."

Over the next few months, Álvaro resodded part of the yard, put down fresh pavers, and brought over more and more orchids, with flowers that looked like dancing girls, grinning monkeys, white egrets in flight. So many years in this house and Felipe had rarely spent time in the yard. All along he had been the owner of a tiny tropical paradise. He could spend hours out there now, marveling at the pink ginger and yellow heliconias that he supposed had always been there.

Maybe that's how a man should spend the twilight of his life, watching flocks of wild parrots jump palm to palm, and breathing the fragrance of the outdoors instead of the grease of that kitchen. Rufi was younger and stronger, and he could run La Rampa better than Felipe these days. Maybe he needed to figure out how to cede the business to Rufi entirely, like the Suwannee brothers had done for him. Felipe had solid savings, a few smart investments. What more could a man want?

"Nobody needs to know what you do on the side," Rosalina had said to him when they were just kids, their parents gunning for them to marry. Felipe had been honorable enough, or weak enough, to remain faithful to her all those years, no matter how his imagination wandered. Now he needed to be man enough, if he wanted to save his relationship with his son. His beautiful son, who was smarter than he, and so much braver.

He dialed Luisito. "I want to stop at your place first and see the art with the paper boats. Do you know I was obsessed with those when I was a boy?"

LYDIA MARTÍN is an award-winning journalist and fiction writer who spent twenty-five years covering Miami's growth and cultural evolution for The Miami Herald. Her writing has appeared in literary journals such as Ploughshares, Fifth Wednesday Journal and Origins Literary Journal; in books such as Presenting Celia Cruz, (Clarkson Potter, 2004) and Louis Vuitton City Guide Miami (LV, 2014); and in magazines such as Billboard, Esquire, InStyle, Oprah, Latina (for which she also served as a contributing editor), Hispanic and Out. She won the 2016 Ploughshares Emerging Writer contest; and the 2016 Editor's Prize from Fifth Wednesday Journal, which nominated her fiction for a Pushcart Prize. Martín, a Yaddo and MacDowell Colony fellow, was part of the Miami Herald team that won a Pulitzer Prize for coverage of 1992's Hurricane Andrew. She was twice a finalist for the Livingston Award, the largest all-media, general reporting prize in American journalism; and won a GLAAD Media Award for Spanish-language magazine writing, among other journalism awards. Martín, born in Havana and raised in Yonkers, Chicago, Flint and Miami, has a BA in English and journalism from the University of Miami (1987) and an MFA in creative writing from Bennington College (2016).

Face-to-Face

Jenna Geisinger

The gift shop, if you could call it that, felt too warm. The soft glow of the windows offended us—our faces skinned down to nerve endings, to muscle and bone. I never cared to see the inside of anyone, and now we were all exposed, naked with our clothes on.

Our faces were our price of admission. The mustached agent ruddied his fingernails with our skin and dumped them like potato peels in the bucket at his feet. The gunk under his nails reminded me of making mud pies with Aileen when we were girls. We delighted in the squish of the mud, the glurp of our hands digging into the earth. It took ages to wash it all off. Ma used a scrub brush and scalding water, taking off our layers until we were pink and new. The water ran black down the drain, but there was still a tiny horseshoe of mud hiding under the cuticles, a reminder of our day in the dirt.

As much as I wanted to hate the shop, it shielded us from the wind. My eyes still burned, but it was a duller ache than outside, where the sea wind mugged us for moisture. Any tears we thought about crying for what we lost turned to caulk, crusting a film over our eyes. Seeing was an act of concentration, a study in patience.

Ignore the dryness and the pounding, the pushpin needling of pain, and focus on what's in front of you.

With a deep focus I looked around the shop and hoped it was a trick of the eyes. At first, the shop seemed to display severed heads in orderly rows by skin shade and gender, some even seemed to wear makeup. I chose one of the heads and stared at it, trying to make sense of it.

They weren't severed heads.

They were faces propped up on mannequin heads, framed by wigs, and primped with blush and lipstick to make them look human. They looked more human than we did with our gnarled mess of muscle and bulging unprotected eyes. I had an urge to touch them, to see if they felt like the thin apple shavings Ma baked for hours with cinnamon that they resembled—Aileen's favorite treat. She liked the snap of them between her teeth.

We heard a scream behind us. A little boy with a bowl cut shrieked as he walked into the shop. His mother tried to pick him up, to soothe him. I couldn't understand what she was saying, but the words were soft and lulling with rounded edges. He screamed louder than her words. He thrashed in her arms, kicking and punching. Most strange was that he couldn't cry. It was a tearless tantrum. There were no reddened cheeks or squinched-up eyes of scared little boys. This was a feral sound. The dried blood and violent shake of his head contorted his hair into snarled brambles. He looked too wild for his corduroy jumper.

A store clerk in her striped red apron adjusted the wigs on the displays. She carefully clipped a section of hair back on one of the mannequins with a barrette from her apron pocket. She stepped back, appraising it. A tendril escaped the clip, and the clerk tucked it back in place. For a moment, she stood there, looking, but I realized the slight smile that played at the corners betrayed her pleasure. She enjoyed staging faces. The clerk turned, sidestepped the screaming boy and the mother desperately trying to calm him, and started work on the window displays, the smile still on her mouth.

As I neared the display the clerk had perfected, I realized the mannequins didn't have eyes. The eyelids bunched and sagged like frayed ribbon. Bored-out eye sockets glared at us from all sides, watching their victims stumble in from the cold.

Ma didn't let us stop at the displays for long. She hustled us to the clearance section at the back of the store. None of this merchandise was groomed. It wasn't even propped up by mannequin heads. These faces were clipped up like pants in department stores and prices tagged their cheeks in bright orange squares. These mugs were morphed and flimsy looking, stretched out from the harsh clips. I wanted to hold out for better, but the air was relentless, digging its claws into the folds of the exposed, picking at them until we begged for coverage. Ma handed me a face with a nose two times the size of my old one.

"That one'd look lovely on you," she said. "Go on, look in the mirror. You'll see."

She used to say that about all the foods I wouldn't try. Aileen and I would cross our arms and refuse to try all kinds of things— brussels sprouts, red cabbage, capers—and Ma'd say, "I know you'd love it if you just gave it a chance." We'd relent, spit them into our napkins. Beets left a violently red stain on cream-colored napkins.

I held the face away from me, using only the very tips of my fingers. The skin was papery in my hands, almost transparent. I finally looked at myself in the mirror, jumping at the reflection. All day I watched the others shuffling through with nerves like the crooked roots of trees, but thought maybe I still looked like me. The mirror mocked the notion, reflecting the dark blood matted into the sides of my hair, the jagged peel-line of skin. I tried to raise my ghost eyebrows, first the left, then the right. The mess of nerve endings and muscle responded. I watched the mass stretch and shift, amazed that this glob of cells belonged to me. The muscles around my mouth strained with dryness when I tried to smile, creaking with the effort. The smile was a mistake. I always thought my teeth were cute, petite, and the slight overlap in the front looked charming. Without lips, they were crowding flowerless tombstones without so much as an epitaph to proclaim they were loved.

"Quit your fooling, and try on the face," Ma said. She already pulled on one that was five shades darker than her old one. There weren't many light-skinned faces on the clearance rack and she wanted to make sure we had ones that were the closest match to our skin. This new face was younger, without all the folds and wrinkles that her old one wore from disarming Aileen's tantrums. Ma stood in the middle of the clearance section with her eyes closed for whole seconds, relishing that she could. The color of the skin blued her eyes into sapphires when she opened them again. It was as strange to see her with a face as it was to see her without one.

Aileen stood behind her, already dressed to kill in an olive number with thick eyebrows and a strong nose that looked digni-fied on her. Aileen's was hardest to look at. How could she still be my sister without the drizzle of freckles or the scar skimming her cheekbone from the sledding accident? She sported someone else's scar on her forehead now—a deep nick above the eyebrows. She examined the tag on the face in the mirror, jumping and fist-pumping like her team won. The tag was marked down because of the damage.

"It's barely a scratch, and it's half off! America's unbelievable," she shouted.

If I could have rolled my eyes, I would have. "That's a stretch," I said, smoothing my new face on, pressing out the wrinkles and wobbly parts with my hands. Getting the eyelids to sit right was the tricky part. The eyelashes kept catching and rolling under.

"I told you, you'd look lovely," Ma said.

Once I got the eyelids adjusted, I closed my eyes too. The stinging stopped immediately. But when I opened them again, the mirror showed someone else. My bloodied hair, but someone else's nose, oversized and goofy. It crowded out everything else. The teeth looked more normal under the awning of pink lips, but these lips were much straighter than the ones I used to know. Constellations of acne stretched across the cheeks in the mirror. I knew I was looking at myself, but just in case, I raised my eyebrows. To my dismay, they responded—sort of. I didn't have the face fitted yet, so it wasn't sitting exactly right.

If only you could spit faces into napkins, but Ma's eyes were welling up. She clasped her hands together like she caught a bird, cupping it closed between her palms. She did that when we found the blue dress for the dance on the clearance rack. That dance ended with my best friend Maebh and me drinking watery punch by the snack table, waiting for the night to finally be over. Thomas Finnegan chose Aoife and they kissed behind the parish while the loud music thumped to the rhythm of my heart splintering. Not that I was still thinking about Thomas ensnared in Aoife's bear-trap mouth. That happened somewhere else, and now we were in America. Now we could be other people.

Ma brushed my hair out of my face with her hands, combing the blood behind my ears. "It'll all be okay now," she said.

"Can we wear faces out of the store?" Aileen asked, face dreamy and far-off.

"Ai, they're not knickers. I think it's a different policy," I said, punching her arm.

For a moment it felt good to joke, as if none of this were real.

"Best check out before the line gets any longer," Ma said, pushing us toward the front of the shop.

*   *   *

The line snaked through the female-face sections of the store and into the male section. We were by the tanner, wider-jawed faces. Mustaches and beards were glued to the upper lips of these creatures, whose emptied sockets were illusions that tricked you into feeling like you were falling aimlessly, forever, with a target always out of reach.

The hordes of the faceless kept pushing into the gift shop after their inspections, covering their heads with their hands. They shoved through the line to get to the various displays, and we simply stepped back to let them through with a curt smile, thankful we were no longer victims to the open air.

We in the line watched them, the faceless, browsing through the displays. We watched their muscles curl in concentration to read the little tags, then we watched them fall, slack, disappointed. The faceless hunched over and kept on to the middle of the store, then, dejected, to the clearance rack. They started to frenzy there like savage raccoons on suburban trash cans, fighting over the unwanted.

Two gift-shop clerks stood just outside of the ravage. The low grumble of human effort, of arms and legs clawing and kicking, permeated, and the two waited, like they were waiting for the rain to slow. The male clerk pushed the woman behind him, and grabbed the first person he could get his hands on, tossing them to the side. And he continued, reading the people with his whole body, moving with the frenzy, then jumping into it, and pulling someone else out of the fight. It was a carnival game to him. I could picture it all. His date behind him, licking at the edges of her ice-cream cone while she cheered, hoping he could win her the biggest bear. He rolled up his sleeves, smiled at her, and joined the game, playing without any real strategy. It seemed almost funny, watching him pounce wildly on an old woman whose knobbed fingers clutched one half of a face. She cried out, but he dragged her to the side. The skin on her arms started to purple before he was even back in the fight.

The man looked back at the other clerk, smiling, as he rerolled his drooping shirtsleeves, already stained with sweat. He was breathing heavy, but you could tell he was just getting started, that dizzy out-of-breath when the thrill starts to build. He was determined to win at the game he started. He winked at her and turned back to the flailing limbs and snarls, pouncing on a teenaged boy.

The muscles in the boy's face peeled from it like old paint. He twisted on the ground, scream-singing a song with a simple melody. His voice haunted the shouts and grunts coming from the fight, his agony an eerie soundtrack.

No one in the line moved. We watched. We watched the aproned clerk tackle people to the ground—the elderly woman, bruised and moaning, and the boy still screaming a song so tinged with comforting we couldn't look him in his red-streaked eyes. We were silent as a little girl was dragged by the undertow of the fight because she wouldn't let go of her mother's leg. The last we saw of her were those blue ribbons that secured her braided pigtails. We stayed at our posts, the line shifting forward as each person reached the cashier.

JENNA GEISINGER is a fiction writer from South Jersey, whose work has appeared in Philadelphia Stories. She is currently pursuing an MFA from William Paterson University and volunteers as assistant editor for the Schuylkill Valley Journal. She is working on a historical fiction novel set in Prohibition-era New York City.

An English Woman and an Arab Man Walk into a Bar

H. de C.

We sit in a circle and the workshop moderator asks us to open our right hand. She goes around, the white gauze of her tunic trailing behind her, placing a dark, wrinkled object the size of an M&M on each cupped hand. She asks us to pretend we don't know what it is. To go sensorial—something I ask my students to do with their essays—to sharpen our senses and experience this "unknown" object with our eyes, nose, ears, and fingers. It's a raisin. A jumbo raisin. I look at it and think of ways to describe it to someone who has never seen one, but my mind betrays me and instead of focusing on the object in front of me, my synapses draw parallels. Does this look like the remains of a charred body? A burnt finger? A toe sizzling in the sun? A nose reduced to twisted cartilage? An ear consumed by flames? A tongue engulfed by salvage fire?

What does it look like? the moderator asks. She walks in and out of the circle gathering answers. The other women have evocative images to share with the group. I'm in a mindfulness workshop.

I'm supposed to be receptive and light, but all I have on my mind right now is two screenshots I have saved on my computer.

In one, a man appears in a collage of four photographs. He is tall, dark, strong, handsome. The first picture of the collage is a selfie shot, in it, he stands in front of a mirror and is dressed in full Arab garb, white tunic, headgear, his cell phone in hand. He looks regal. In the other two, he is showing off his brown muscular arms and fine physique, he is a beautiful man. The next shot is of him dressed in a fancy black dress shirt, something a young man would wear to the club. From the pictures I know this about him: he is an Arab man, in his early thirties, he wears black-rim glasses and he is strong. Very strong.

The other screenshot is also a collage, this time of pictures of a young woman. She is petite, white, delicate, pretty. In one picture she is with a girlfriend, they are laughing and toasting. She exudes youth, fun, joie de vivre. She wears a sparkly miniskirt and high heels. Her straight black hair falls right above her shoulders, the light from the flash gives her hair an outwardly glow. In another shot, she is with an attractive blond woman, her mom. They are looking at each other and laughing. In another picture, the camera catches her at an angle. She sits sideways, knees together, legs crossed at the ankles, a smile beams across her face. She looks happy. From the pictures I know this about her: she is Caucasian, in her late twenties, slim and short and loves a good party. She looks like a gust of wind could sweep her off her feet. She looks fragile.

*   *   *

The jumbo raisin in my hand is the size of an eight-week-old fetus. Imagine that. Toes and fingers still webbed. Eyes still shut. Heart beating at around 150 times per minute. Lips and tongue still a guess. Life, such an uncertain journey. The moderator asks us to touch the raisin. To caress it. To become acquainted with its ridges, and squishiness. *Squishiness*, such a childish word. I place the raisin between my thumb and index fingers and press a little, just enough to change its shape, to test its malleability, its willingness to surrender. What does it feel like? she wants us to ponder. Like an open wound, I think.

* * *

Qatar, October 2013. An English teacher and her French girl-friend walk into Sky View, a nightclub on the rooftop of a hotel. They are dressed to impress. Their plan is simple: get a few fruity cocktails, dance to whatever the DJ has in store, smash that popular song with killer moves, turn a few heads, take pictures with Doha's skyline in the background, post them on Instagram and Facebook, make a few girly trips to the toilet to correct smeared mascara or reapply lipstick, take a taxi at the end of the night, sit in the back of the cab and look at the pictures they just took at the club. Laugh. Slap each other in the arms. *Stop it. It wasn't like that. No way. OMG. Delete that one.* Get home, crash on the couch. *Best night ever.*

Maybe not. Maybe their plan is to walk into the club, survey the patrons, make eye contact with the ones they like, let them pay for their drinks. Sure, a Cosmopolitan would be lovely. Thank you. Do I want to dance? Of course, I want to dance. A little twerking with a stranger has never hurt anyone. The night is young, they are young, a river of daiquiris, piña coladas, Negronis, dry martinis, and Moscow mules runs wild that night. The young teachers bathe in it. A little smooch here and there. Not too much. *Easy, cowboy. Keep your hands to yourself. Men are such pigs.*

Same country, same night. An Arab man and his friend also walk into the club. They are locals and as such, they are not allowed to wear their national dress—long white tunics and headwear—where alcohol is served. The men walk in smelling of cologne, sporting expensive jeans, designer shirts, and trendy shoes. Their plan is simple: get a few beers, maybe a few whiskies, dance to whatever the DJ has in store for the night, hit on a few women, see what happens, take pictures, post them on Instagram and Facebook, smoke a couple of cigars, drive home with the windows of their SUV rolled down, blast Arab music through their Bose speakers, steer the wheel with one hand, feel badass.

Maybe not. Maybe their plan is to walk into the club, get ham-mered, hit on any pretty Westerner—*white women are so easy*—and see what happens. Maybe their plan is to sit at the bar and stalk their prey. Wait until the pretty blond gets drunk and dry-hump her on the dance floor. Maybe their plan is to follow her to the bathroom and have her from behind as she bends over the toilet to vomit one too many martinis.

*   *   *

Breathe the raisin in, the moderator says. Inhale it like your life depends on this breath. Is it odorless? Is it sweet? Have you smelled anything like it before? I close my eyes, bring the raisin to my nose, and take a long lungful of air. Nothing. I don't smell anything. I think of the futility of this exercise. Of the different ways I could have spent one hundred dollars and three hours of my weekend. It is, after all, a workshop on mindfulness, a course to teach me how to be in the moment, to ground my body and mind in the present, right here, right now, in this posh yoga studio overlooking the ocean, surrounded by wealthy women who, unlike me, have obedient minds that focus and produce all sort of poetic words to describe their raisins.

*   *   *

The Arab Man spots The English Teacher across the dance floor. They'd met before. Once or twice. Maybe at someone's party or at a BBQ in the desert. Yeah, they liked each other. The guy was cool—she remembers. The girl was hot—he remembers. They introduce their friends and they dance and drink with abandon, tonight is a dreamed life finally come true. One a.m., last orders. C'mon, seriously? *Booo*, they want the party to go on forever. *No problem*, The Man says, *the party is on chez moi*. The girls look at each other. Why the hell not? They are tipsy and high on life. They get into his SUV, but soon the French girl changes her mind. She wants to go home. She is tired and ready for bed. The English Teacher is on fire. *Fine, suit yourself. I'll party alone.* They drop

off the French teacher. they kiss goodbye. *You okay?* They ask
each other in unison. *Cool as a cucumber. I'll call you tomorrow.
Bye. Partaayy!*

* * *

I imagine the following day. A lonely falconer is out in the desert
scouting for bird-training grounds. He is a Bedouin. A man hard-
ened by life in the desert, with a face battered by cold winter winds
and mean summer sandstorms; a man fluent in the language of
birds of prey, thoroughly acquainted with a falcon's razor-sharp
claws digging into his arm; a man who has seen it all and heard it
all. One could say, an unimpressionable man. He spots smoke
rising into the air a few yards in front of him, looks for evidence
of a campsite and finds none. He walks toward the billows of
smoke propelled by sheer curiosity but stops abruptly at the edge
of the pit. The unimpressionable man gasps, invokes Allah with
broken utterances, grabs his head with both hands, then covers
his nose as he peeks into the pit. Whatever is still burning smells
like bad weather, like a rain of locusts, like the end of the world
and everything that's precious in it. Whatever is still burning smells
like heartbreak and tears. Like the phone call no mother ever wants
to receive. Like the deafening silence that follows the unthinkable
words: *are you such and such's mother? We are sorry to inform you
that . . .*

I imagine The English Teacher's Mother picking up the phone
in England, trying to make sense of the words uttered over the
phone. Someone is calling from the other side of the world to let
her know about a body found in the desert.

What's that have to do with me?

It's urgent, the voice says.

What? What do you mean? Who are you again?

Something about identifying human remains.

Her hand on her chest. She can't remember how to breathe.

Remains? Whose remains? What kind of sick joke is this?

They think it's her daughter.

Yes, my daughter is a teacher. She teaches children in Qatar.
Then she hears words, not full sentences, but only disjointed
words:
Burnt.
DNA.
Beyond identification.
Body.
Dental records.
Then the inexplicable eclipse. Her presence is required.
The lights go off.
Darkness takes over.

*   *   *

I imagine the look on her face the following day when she arrives
at the Hamad Mortuary in Doha. Her disbelief. Her reluctance
to accept that these charred remains are her daughter. *Where is
her face so she can kiss it? Where are her lips? Where did the eyes go?
What happened to her legs?* She thinks about walking away. She
would refuse to identify the remains and would not leave the
country until her real daughter, the whole of her, is returned.
Then they would fly back to England and that would be the end
of it. What a cruel mishap, to make her fly all the way there to
identify the wrong body. But she can't identify her daughter, not
just because she is grief-stricken and in denial, but because what
was left of the body weighs only 7.5 kilograms. As heavy as a
gallon of paint. A Jack Russell. Three bricks. Her daughter is a
collection of disassembled body parts: a chunk of her skull, a
portion of her neck, the braces on her upper jaw teeth, a section
of her chest with a twenty-centimeter knife still lodged in her
ribs, and the feet, my God, the feet. They are intact, not through
an act of mercy, but because the men had dumped her body
headfirst into the firepit, sparing her feet from the flames. Her
toenails are painted red. How odd. The mother recognizes the
red nail polish. The weight on her chest is unbearable. She is all
tremors and tears. She is disheveled and infinitely cold, so cold.
She feels like screaming, like putting fists through walls, like

tearing her clothes off, like putting her rapturous rage to good use. This mother, unhinged by grief, needs an explanation. She wants to know whose ribs she is looking at and who put the knife there. Such a vulgar anachronism. She wants to know who turned her daughter into this burnt changeling: a child stolen by desert spirits.

* * *

My mother's death is the greatest loss I have suffered so far. Grief hit me hard, made me, some people said, catatonic, unable to write anything worth keeping. Instead of writing, I read. A lot. Research was my coping mechanism of choice. I read everything I found about postmortem bodies. Livor, rigor and algor mortis, cremation, the disintegration of that soft body where I dwelt the first nine months of my life. I honored her life by digging deep into her death and all its gory details. Intellectualizing her death brought me unimaginable peace and acceptance. After the viewing (I refused to look at her dead body) and the mass, my siblings and I took her body to the crematorium where we surrendered her to the technicians. This is what happened to her after we left her there: she was moved out of the coffin and placed inside a combustible container—what do crematoria do with the caskets?—where her body was reduced to its basic elements at about sixteen hundred degrees Fahrenheit inside a cremation chamber called retort. The heat dried her up, burned her skin and hair, contracted and charred the muscles, vaporized the soft tissues, and calcified the bones until they crumbled. I stood outside the crematorium and stared at the exhaust system waiting for the smell of mom's charred flesh and the sight of smoke. I got neither. The emissions system is designed to destroy the smoke and vaporize the gases that would produce any smell. Did you know that the skull is the bone structure that takes longest to incinerate? Sometimes, a cremation technician must use a hoe-like rod to crush it. I assume this operation was included in the cremation fees. Maybe, unbeknownst to us, my siblings and I paid someone to crush our mother's skull to pieces before we sent her to the cremulator, a machine where her bones were pulverized into a finer sand-like consistency. The disintegration of her body took about three hours. Her fleshy dark lips, her soft hips, her generous belly, all her life-giving body reduced to a mere five pounds of pasty white powder called *cremains*. Sometimes I lay in bed and think of mom's bones in full *pugilistic attitude*, the medical term used to describe the postmortem involuntary clenching of hands into fists and the flexion of elbows, knees, hip, and neck caused by muscles contracting when the body is exposed to extremely high temperatures. Mom in a full boxer's stance before becoming dust. Mom ready to throw a final punch as the cremation technician raised the hoe aiming at her skull.

*　*　*

You haven't said much, the moderator says looking at me. I shake my head and let her know, without words, that I don't want to speak. That's okay, she says softly, like I have admitted to an embarrassing shortcoming. She doesn't know that it's the fifth anniversary of The English Teacher's death and I'm caught in a moment of inexplicable grief. I think of how we teach our daughters to be on guard, to be aware of the dangers lurking in college, at the nightclub, in the boy's car, to be always on the ready, pepper spray handy, to avoid dark alleyways and talking to strangers. *Sharpen your elbows, baby girl. Push. Shove. Kick them where it hurts. Scream. Bite. Scratch. Blow your whistle. Do not open the door. Do not get into his car. Do not let him pay for your drink. Do not leave your drink unattended. Do not park your car next to a van. Take self-defense classes. Learn to earn their respect one uppercut at a time. Do not party too hard. Do not get hammered. Do not send mixed signals. Men are easily misled, and you know, boys will be boys.* And speaking of boys, what do parents tell their boys?

I want to focus on the exercise. I want to ground myself, connect to this group of strangers and simply be, but when the moderator asks us to bring the raisin to our ear and describe what we hear, I close my eyes and think of crackling bones. Dry twigs burning on a fire. Autumn leaves crunched under one's weight. Sparks. A Fourth of July of the body. I rely heavily on metaphors because I don't have the right words to describe a pain that's not mine. A phone call that I didn't receive. The death of a young woman I never met. The language of emotion is too simple, the ABCs of being alive, to describe somebody else's pain. So, I resort to using figurative language, looking inside its vastness for the words I need to imagine the crime itself and the pain that ensued.

*   *   *

The newspapers didn't say much. They ran timid news on the crime, the only homicide in the country in several years, then they stopped reporting. Life quickly went back to what it was before: activities at the souk, fashion shows, visiting diplomats, new restaurants, brand-new hotels, lavish brunches, soft and grand shopping-mall openings. So much to see and do. Better not give the readers the wrong impression. After all, it is one of the safest countries in the world. A nation with no history of bank robberies, muggings, break-ins, or stolen vehicles. No drug dealers ruining neighborhoods, drive-by shootings, or street gangs. Why destroy that image with gory details about a single crime? The country needs Western technology, expertise, English teachers, let them come. No need to scare them away. This was an isolated event. There were almost eighteen thousand British citizens living in the country in 2013. One dead Briton out of eighteen thousand equals 0.0055 percent, all those invalidating zeros to the left. The expat community spoke about it at coffee breaks and executive lunches. Over Friday bubbly and happy hour at the Ritz. *Poor thing. Have you seen her Facebook page? All miniskirts and booze. Was he her boyfriend? Maybe she was pregnant and that's why he killed her. I hope she didn't suffer. Oh, God, I hope she was dead when they set her on fire. C'mon, she knew what she was doing when she got in the car with two Arab men. You don't wear a miniskirt in a Muslim country for God's sake. Was she really wearing a miniskirt? Was she drunk? There you go. What do you expect?*

*   *   *

Soon after the falconer discovered her body, both Arab men were apprehended. The Friend accepted a plea bargain: he pleaded guilty to aiding in the disposal of her body and gave a full confession in exchange for three years behind bars. Three years, the same sentence for a third DUI in the state of Connecticut. The Friend's confession satisfied the jury. The men drove The Teacher to an apartment. They drank. The Man took her into a room to have sex with her. The Friend didn't touch her, he claimed. Sometime later, The Man came out of the room in shock begging his friend for help. He had stabbed The English Teacher twice. She was dead. They drove her body to the outskirts of the city, dumped it into a pit near a farm, and set it ablaze.

* * *

"We tell ourselves stories in order to live," Joan Didion wrote. I think she meant, we need answers, motives, a meaningful existence filled with meaningful moments. The wounded people—family and friends—and the rest of us, wanted to know why. The tragedy was easier to understand if we knew a reason: lust, jealousy, hatred, revenge, any emotional tenor commensurate with the savagery of the act. His lawyers claimed self-defense. A five foot five petite woman allegedly attacked a strong man towering over her and he stabbed her in a moment of self-preservation. The defense argued at various times that he was mentally incapable at the time of the murder and that their client had been interrogated by police without a lawyer. On an occasion, the defense claimed that The Teacher had committed suicide.

* * *

The court refused to use the word *rape*, and so did the local newspapers. It was reported that The Teacher had been *conquered*. Conquered. The irony. She was raped and stabbed on October 12, the day that Columbus conquered the New World. One could talk about Columbus's rape of America, but one could not talk about the conquest of The Teacher.

Semantics.

conquer *(verb)*

from Old French *conquerre*, based on Latin *conquirere* "gain, win," from con- an expression of completion + *quaerere* "seek"

Definition

1 : to overcome and take control of (a place or people) by military force.

2 : to successfully overcome a problem or weakness.

3 : to climb (a mountain) successfully.

4 : to gain the love, admiration, or respect for a person or group of people.

No, no and a thousand times no. The English Teacher was not conquered.

*   *   *

A few years ago, I contacted The Teacher's Mother. I was writing a chapter for a book about the repatriation of human remains and wanted to interview her. We met at a hotel, hugged lightly, looked into each other's eyes without either mentioning her daughter, ordered tea, and talked about the weather, the traffic, her trips to appear in court—almost twenty, the ignominy of it all. How when she goes to court, she grabs a number and stands in a queue to be heard by a jury of men. How she has to stand there and listen as her interpreter translates everyone's grievances: a stolen laptop from someone's room in a work camp, a mobile phone left in a cab, a landlord increasing the rent beyond what's stipulated by the law, a work visa that can't be transferred, unpaid salaries, a poisoned dog, then her voice: my daughter was raped, stabbed to death, and set ablaze, your honor, followed by other pitiful grievances. It wasn't just the perversity of what had been done to her daughter, it was also the humiliation of the circus-like court proceedings. There was the reenactment of the crime for which she flew in. In the recreation, The Teacher was played by a male actor. She raged in silence. The prosecution complained. The scene showed two men of about the same height and weight scuffling. It didn't represent the disparity in height and weight between The Man and The Teacher. A new hearing was scheduled, and she flew back home. Later she flew back to Doha for the "real" reenactment. The same movie was shown in court. No new reenactment had been produced. She went back to the UK, deflated, humiliated but undeterred. She came back for another day of court proceedings. This time, due to technical difficulties, no audiovisual equipment was available, and a tiny laptop had to be brought in for the jury. Unfortunately, the laptop had run out of power and the lead was not long enough to reach the socket from the juror's table. She had to go home with no answers. A few months later she bought another round-trip ticket to Qatar. For the umpteenth time, she went home empty-handed and again and again ad infinitum.

I didn't want to sound trite. What I wanted was to have the ability to offer her something substantial, not another *I'm sorry for your loss*, although I was, still am, terribly sorry for her loss. What I wanted was an impossibility: to have the power to save her the indignity of standing in line as if her daughter's murder was another petty misdemeanor, to have this solution she hadn't thought of, the *wasta*, influence, to expedite the process and give her the only thing close to closure: The Man's execution. But I had nothing of value to offer; instead, I asked imprudent questions about the repatriation of her daughter's remains. She gave me nothing. Afraid of interfering with the process, she had stopped talking to the press or anyone outside family and friends. A self-imposed gag order of sorts. We hugged goodbye and I watched her walk away. It hurt to watch the fluency of a body acclimated to grief.

*   *   *

I have been staring at the raisin and thinking of The Teacher for so long that I have lost all interest in the workshop. The moderator instructs us to put it in our mouths, but not chew it. Not yet.

It's a lesson on delaying gratification, an invitation to experience rather than to simply eat the raisin. My stomach turns. I place this eight-week-old fetus in my mouth, webbed toes and all, this charred pinky, this burnt big toe and sob. A quiet sob. I can't get this girl out of my mind. This girl, two years younger than my own daughter, this girl who reminds me of me and my own traveling dreams when I was twenty-four, this girl who trusted two men and died at their hands. When I'm not thinking of her last minutes, I'm thinking about her mom. Sometimes I even think of the other grieving mother. The Man is somebody else's son. There has been another heartbroken mother on the other side of the courtroom. Another mother looking at her child and praying for leniency, for another year, one more Ramadan, one more Eid, a mother fighting for his life. The irony is that The Teacher's Mother doesn't want The Man to die either. She'd much rather see him get old behind bars, have the certainty he will never see the sunrise again. But that's not a choice. She either forgives him, and he walks, or she doesn't, and he gets the death penalty. On a few occasions during the hearings, The Teacher's Mother crossed paths with The Man as she came out of the restroom. She looked into his dark eyes, the same pair of eyes her daughter must have stared into as he raped her, and later, while he drove the knife beyond her skin as if looking for her heart. The amount of self-restraint it must have taken her to look at him and not attack him. What mantras did she repeat in her head to keep her fingernails from scratching the skin on his face or gouge his eyes? How hard did she bite her tongue and bleed inside the mouth to drown all the expletives she knew, to not spit her fury on the chest guarding his still-beating heart?

*   *   *

After the raisin activity, we have the hand-shadow exercise. The purpose of this activity has something to do with trust and focus. We pair up. I have one of the women attending the workshop in front of me. She moves her left hand in the air drawing circles and soft *s*'s here and there. I follow her with my right hand, our palms close to each other but not quite touching. My job is to focus and somehow guess the trajectory of the woman's hand, anticipate the next move. I discover this is much easier if instead of her hand, I focus on her eyes. Our hands are now in the periphery doing their own dance while we lock gazes. The woman appears to be in her fifties, is blond, white, attractive, and has eloquent blue yes. She looks oddly familiar. There is tenderness in this stranger's eyes, something akin to pain and for a moment it feels as though I know what she needs, and I want to give it to her. Our hands are great dance partners. An uncanny connection binds me to her eyes. Her hand moves fast, then slow, then fast again. I'm right here with it. She moves her hand toward my chest, mine hovers over hers and as she moves her hands toward her heart, she starts to cry. I cry with her. Neither says a word. We let the tears run in silence as we take turns following each other's hands. And with misty eyes, I realize why she looks familiar. She looks like The Teacher's Mother. Or maybe she doesn't. Maybe the only thing they have in common is skin color and nationality and the other parallels are figments of my imagination. But there we were, mother to mother, woman to woman, standing in front of each other, our hands guiding us into each other's hearts.

*   *   *

The outlandish defense arguments didn't hold any water. In 2014, he was sentenced to death. In 2015, his death sentence was upheld. In 2016, after countless court hearings, his sentence was overturned, the verdict was thrown out, and a retrial began. In 2017, a judged asked The Teacher's Mother whether she wanted to forgive or seek financial retribution against her daughter's rapist and killer. No, she didn't want to forgive him and no, she didn't want blood money. For the second time, The Man was sentenced to death, which was to be carried out by firing squad or hanging. I wonder if she had any preference. Then came 2018, The Teacher's Mother made her trip number thirty to Qatar to attend judgement day, to hear from the judge's mouth when the death sentence would be carried out. Only the defense team had appealed again and had managed to get his death sentence reduced to ten years in jail.

He has already served five.

He'll be out after Qatar hosts the 2022 World Cup.

* * *

After we finish the hand-shadow activity, the moderator asks each pair to sit on the floor, back to back, to turn our faces and whisper to our partners what the hand-shadow experience had been like. My blue-eyed partner goes first. She thanks me for having been so receptive, for allowing her *in* without reservations. She tells me how lovely it was to feel so close to a complete stranger and share those few seconds of mutual recognition. Then it is my turn.

As I sit there, my back against her back, our tired wombs placidly resting between our legs crossed in lotus, and being as honest as I can, I whisper: *I'm so sorry for your loss.* The woman nods as if accepting my condolences, which makes me wonder if she has lost someone too. My mind wanders off and I imagine that my back is leaning against The Mother's back.

* * *

Dear Mother,

You are not alone. It only feels that way. There is a large, rowdy tribe of women hungry for justice. Nothing will take away the pain, no one will replace your daughter, not a day will go by that you don't wish she were alive, but life will go on. Inexplicably. Stubbornly. The sun will rise every morning and with it the promise of blue skies, dewdrops, tides, and rain, which means butterflies, bees, trees, flowers, and rivers. The ugly stuff too, of course. Sandstorms, avalanches, floods, volcanic eruptions, destruction, death. Your grief won't stop your neighbor's kids from laughing outside or your friends from having sex. Despite the vulgarity of our quotidian lives, there will be Christmases and stores sales, books and songs will be written, the animal kingdom will continue to birth more humans and more animals, which is both reassuring and terrifying. And when the earth's rotational cycle is all over, the sun will rise again, and yes, you will have no option but to make the best of that single day without her. You will have no option but to make it all the way to nightfall and whether you do this on your knees or your feet it's up to you.

Every mother who gives birth to a daughter holds dual citizenship: one in the kingdom of her own womb, which is sacred but limited to a few months where the daughter is queen, and one in the kingdom of the world, which is mysterious, dangerous, dissonant, and finite where the daughter is nothing but a grain of sand. You will move back and forth between the two kingdoms, the twenty-four-year span when she was a hug and a kiss away. And this space between fury and despair will eventually be filled with love. The kind that comes at you like an uninvited guest and leaves you trembling with gratitude. Love like jazz riffs, sharp and pungent one minute; wary and saccharine the next. Life will go on. For you, for me, and for every woman who gives birth or is birthed into this world. We need life to go on so that every day we can fight for equality, safety, and justice. This much, I know.

Naturally, I don't say any of this to the woman whose back I'm leaning mine against. Instead, I turn my face in her direction to whisper what I think she needs to hear, but before I utter a word, she grabs hold of a few of my fingers on the floor and sobs quietly. We lock pinkies like little girls and stay like this until the workshop is over.

H. DE C. is a teacher who loves to travel. A traveler who loves to dance. A dancer who loves to write. H. de C. has written a couple of books and several essays, some of which have won numerous awards and honors.

Fear

Divya Sood

There is a fruit stand by NYU, two hundred and sixty-nine and one half steps away from the edge of Washington Square Park, sixty-nine steps to the left of The Dosa Man's cart. There is nothing spectacular about the stand itself except that you can buy lychees there. And the lychees are so sweet and their flesh is so soft, they remind me of the lychees in Calcutta.

When they talk, my parents always say I was raised in Calcutta. This may be so and I do remember tiffin carriers filled with steaming rice and lukewarm fish. I remember canteen bottles that tried so hard to keep filtered water cool. But I also know within myself that even though I went to school there and played hopscotch in dusty allies, it is New York that raised me. It is here that my senses were heightened to possibility. So much so I believe that when they say I am crazy and fill out a diagnosis form that I don't ever have the chance to see, I want to say, "I'm not crazy. You just don't see what I see. You never woke up. I did. In fact, waking up is the only transgression of my mind."

I often want to scream, "Loving her is the only transgression of my heart. Losing her is the only tragedy of my life."

And sometimes, when it is dark and I stare out of the window at the shapes of trees shaking ominously in a cold wind, I know my worst transgression is waking up every morning and wanting to die.

Maybe what makes people crazy is shards of a broken heart that somehow reach the brain and cause chaos. Or perhaps people lose sanity when they realize life is dismissive of what we hold most precious and so it takes and takes even if we are not ready to give.

Nights like these I fully believe that she is alive. I call her and she does answer her phone. I remember the first time, and the second time as well if I think about it, that I was at Bellevue. She had come to see me every day. And yet she does not come here. Has she believed the voices that echo like useless wind speaking to mute trees? Has she listened to the voices say, "She is not worthy of you. She will not ever understand life the way you do. Stay away." Could it be that she has finally believed them?

I am standing in front of the window facing darkness. In the glass, I see his reflection. He is behind me, the goofy nurse whose job is to make sure I don't kill myself in the middle of the night. His name is Tony. His goatee looks almost orange under the fluorescent lights. He has slicked back his hair and it shines. And in the glass, his reflection looks surreal, as if he is a vision more than a reality.

"Can't sleep," I say.

I don't even turn around.

"Do you want something for that?" he asks.

"No more pills! Please, for God's sake, no more pills, okay?"

"Okay."

"You're very tall," I say.

"Six four," he says.

He comes behind me and touches my shoulder gently.

"Do you want to talk?" he says.

I sigh.

"It might help," he says.

I turn to face him, his blue eyes trying to make sense of me. I have often stared at myself through my own gray eyes in mirrors and reflecting windows and have never been able to figure myself out. I wish he could know he's wasting his time. Eventually, I think, he will learn.

He motions toward the spare chair in the room, walks to it, then sits down. They did not allow me to have a roommate. Not as if I wanted one anyway. I have never understood how they can deem you crazy and then make you share your bedroom with another crazy person. But what the hell do I know? I've spent seventy-nine days here at St. Vincent's of Westchester and I still don't understand most of it. And there is more to come.

"What are you thinking about?" he asks.

"My girlfriend. I am thinking about why she has not come to see me."

"So you're like a lesbian, huh? No shit."

Have you ever wondered why people would blame you if you hit an idiot?

"You're too pretty," he continues. "Your hair is amazing. I love long hair with waves."

"Wavy hair?" I ask.

"Yeah. And you're gorgeous."

"My girlfriend is more beautiful than I am," I say.

He doesn't say anything.

"She won't pick up her phone though," I say, "otherwise she'd come visit me. She always does. I've been in these hospitals twice. And she used to come every day."

"Alisha," he says.

The taunting in his voice is gone and he sounds somber.

"Alisha, when is the last time you saw her?"

"Eighty days ago."

"Tell me about it."

My mind races through corridors. It is as if I do not want to tell him and as if I am confused. But I remember exactly where I saw her. I remember that her hands were cold and frail.

"She was in the hospital," I say.

"Why, Alisha?"

"I don't know."

I look at him and he doesn't move. Again those blue eyes search me and try to force me to travel to pasts I do not want to remember.

"She had leukemia, you dick. All right? She died there. Are you happy?"

"No. No, Alisha. This isn't about me. It's about you. How do you feel?"

My voice is uneven, like a cup and saucer held by trembling hands.

"Fuck you," I whisper.

"Easy there," he says as he rises from his chair.

"Fuck you," I say more softly.

I wait for him to speak.

"Sometimes she is alive, Tony, all right? Sometimes I know she is alive and everyone is lying. Why is that so hard for you to believe?"

"Because she is dead, Alisha, and the faster you can accept that, the sooner they will let you out of here."

"I don't even know if I care. I don't want to live a life."

"What about your parents?" he says as if I haven't said anything at all.

"My parents think I am insane because of her. They won't come here."

"That must be rough."

"If I gave a fuck, yes. I don't."

He settles back in his chair.

It is as if the conversation about her is lost in the cold night outside my window and we sit here like drinking buddies, talking about sports and good fucks instead of life and death and loss. Sometimes, I do not believe that she has died. I have not even cried for her. They tell me I must understand that she is dead and I must cry, grieve for her. I tell them to fuck off.

I do not want to talk to Tony anymore. I go back to my window and stare into darkness, the trees conversing among themselves, the leaves swaying so violently, I feel they understand my heart.

My heart remembers the taste of rosewater upon her lips. My heart remembers her voice and is afraid every second of every minute of every hour of every day that it will forget the intonations and cadences of her words. My heart remembers seeing her in a hospital bed, her face dry and brown, her eyes devoid of eyeliner and mascara and the shimmer of eye shadow. And yet she was still my Anjali, beautiful and strong. Despite her frailty, despite her failing blood, she was still my lover, my guide, my best friend.

I have made a friend here. Her name is Vani. She cleans floors and garbage and shit and vomit. She never complains. She is old and dark and she smells like coconut oil. But she is soft and gentle and holds my hand when she talks. She does not question me or what I tell her of Anjali. She does not try to make me feel. Usually, she just slowly shakes her head from side to side whether she agrees or disagrees. She is kind.

At night between one fifty-three and two seventeen, Tony falls asleep in the spare chair. Most nights I walk past him slowly and go to the kitchen where Vani comes to heat her dinner. While she is on her break, we have an hour where we just sit or just talk or just sit and talk.

The first night we meet, I am in the kitchen by myself, hiding from the nurse who is trying to force me to take my meds. She walks in and heats her food without acknowledging me or asking me what I am doing in the kitchen. This bothers me.

"Aren't you going to ask what I'm doing here?" I ask.

She looks at me. She is dark and darker still are the circles under her eyes. Her hair is pulled back and she has a braid that falls to her ass.

"I am not a doctor, ma'am. I am not a nurse. I clean floors and bathrooms. Why would I ask you what you are doing?"

Her accent is thick but comforting, like the accent shared by my parents. Losing your parents to their own stubbornness makes you miss them sometimes. Only sometimes though. Not enough to beg forgiveness for loving or being.

Her gold earrings catch glints of the fluorescent lights. I watch her heat her food: basmati rice and some pungent coconut fish. The smells mingle and the nostalgia of India permeates the room.

She takes her plastic container and a plastic fork and settles into a chair in the corner, by the window, as if she sees something other than bleak darkness outside.

"So you won't tell them I'm in here, then?"

She shakes her head from side to side.

"I don't get involved," she says.

I watch her eat her food. Fork in rice, fork in coconut fish curry, mouth. Again and again.

I imagine her day in and day out, cleaning floors and toilets. Her uniform is clean and pressed but underneath, her maroon sari still pokes through.

"You look like a big lychee!" I say.

She doesn't respond at all. No flinches, no words. Rice, coconut fish curry, mouth.

"I'm a lesbian." I say.

She looks at me.

"Why do you want my attention, Mol?" she says.

I am offended.

"I don't want your attention. I just thought I'd tell you."

"So the next time I clean your floor, will it make a difference? Mol, I work. I eat. I have five children and a lazy husband."

I stare into her vacuous eyes, brown like dark chocolate, unrelenting like the ground in times of no monsoon.

"What if one of your children were gay?" I ask.

"What if? Then what? So what? Mol, there are more important things in life, no? More important than gay or no gay."

"I have a girlfriend," I say. She hasn't come to see me."

She watches me, chocolate-brown eyes looking into my own gray eyes, my eyes full of despair.

"Mol, if she loves you, she will come. Life is not about what or whom we desire but about what or who desires us, no?"

"So she will come then?"

She shakes her head from side to side.

"Yes. Yes."

"What does *Mol* mean?" I ask her.

"You are North Indian, no?"

"Yes."

"*Mol* is South Indian. It is from the language of Malayalam and means 'dear one.'"

I do not know what it is about her but she makes me feel safe. I had felt safe once in my mother's arms when I was hurt or bruised from outside or inside and she held me and told me life was good but not always fair. Now what I remember most vividly of my mother is her turning to leave me the first time I was at Bellevue. She never saw me again. And I hear still her last words, "This woman will destroy you. When you come to your senses, then return to us."

How can you return from love? How can you return from your heart's desire? These questions my mother did not answer before she left. All I know is, I never saw her thereafter. Phone conversations at Diwali and New Year's suffice for us to wish one another a happy time, a wonderful life. Ironic, I know.

I miss you, Ma. Even though. And still. I miss you. I miss hearing you say my name as if it were valuable.

"What is your name?" Vani asks.

"Her name is Anjali," I say. "My name is Alisha Malhotra."

She shakes her head slowly side to side as she says, "Alisha Malhotra."

"Well, goodnight," I say.

I leave her that night as she finishes her rice and coconut curry fish. I walk slowly to my room and all the while have the desire to bury my head in her sari and sleep. I think sometimes when those we love leave us, we are overwhelmed at possibilities that we may be loved again. She makes me miss my mother. And nothing in this universe, even that which we sometimes call God, can change that.

After that first meeting, I go as frequently as I can to watch Vani eat her dinner. There are nights when there is too much noise in my mind and I do not go to see her. But most nights I

do because Vani washes me with a calm that I do not find any-
where else.

As time passes, I think I might tell her that Anjali has died. But
while she heats food and I sit beside her, I enjoy telling her about
Anjali and I enjoy most of all hearing that Anjali will come to see
me. Throughout each day, I vacillate between believing Anjali is
alive and knowing Anjali is not alive. But with Vani, for the hour
that we share, it is so easy to believe that Anjali is alive and that
she will come to see me because Vani is one person who does not
know the truth. And she believes as much as I do, without hesita-
tion or question, that Anjali will come back to me. I do not want
to sacrifice these pleasures.

"She hasn't come to see me," I say.

"Mol, she loves you, no?"

"Yes. Yes. I know a thousand times, yes."

"Then she will."

She strokes my back. Her hand is heavy. Her touch is so comforting it makes me believe. Anjali *will* come.

Anjali does not come.

I spend my days in recreational therapy as if drawing with
pastels or middle C on a piano will heal whatever is broken or
tarnished within me. It doesn't. I divide my heart and mind into
two time zones: times I know Anjali is dead and times I believe
that she is alive. The rest of my time is interference, white noise,
black noise, nothing worth listening to anyway.

One night, a Wednesday, Vani and I are in the kitchen. She
eats her *idli sambar*, mounds of soft rice and golden yellow spicy
lentils, and I watch. She calls me to her.

"Eat, Mol," she says.

She feeds me with a spoon and I feel, above all, safe.

"Tell me about this Anjali."

I lean back and swallow. I sigh. Then I speak.

"I met Anjali on the street during a rainstorm," I say.

"Every great love story has a little rain, no?"

I laugh.

"Ours did. I met her then. We dated. We dared. I was nineteen. She was twenty-six. That day we bought lychees. She had never tasted one. She was raised here, not in India at all. She held two lychees in her palm. 'One is you,' she said. 'One is me.' I fed her lychees that day. Her first lychees. She squeezed them in her palms until her fingertips held the fragrance of their pulpy flesh. That is the day I fell in love. That is the day everything changed. Some good. Some terrible."

"My name is Vani," she offers.

It is enough of an offering.

As of then, we are friends.

I talk to Vani as often as I can.

I am grateful for Tony's naps.

There are times we meet that I am not in the mood to talk. Last night was one of those times. It wasn't for anything that happened or that Vani did. I was just tired of believing one thing and knowing another and then sometimes believing and knowing the same thing. I wanted some peace. And I wanted the courage to tell Vani the truth.

"Anjali still hasn't come," I say.

"Mol, she will come," Vani says.

"How do you know?" I say.

"I know."

"Maybe you don't want her to come because you're like everyone else; you don't believe this is real. No girl and no boy and we are not real to you because we are Indian and this is not how we do things."

Vani is quiet.

"Say something."

"Mol, I can say no more than not all people are the same. Yes, I am sorry for your mother and your father. But me, gay no gay, no difference. Believe me or don't."

I look into the fake mirror on the wall. I call it fake because it is not glass for obvious reasons. And because it is not glass, it distorts everything as if it has a right to rephrase reality.

My hair is oily. I haven't washed it for a week now. But still, it is long and black and wavy. My skin looks dull but then why shouldn't it? I feel muted myself. Maybe it's the meds. Maybe it's my soul. I no longer know the difference.

"Then why won't she come?" I whisper.

I turn around and our eyes meet. Vani touches my cheek with her hand. Her fingers are rough. Too many dishes washed, too many bathrooms cleaned.

"I don't know, Mol. I don't know. But she will. Trust me."

I hug her. I feel for a moment that my mother has returned, devoid of anger, full of the love she once gave and I once knew.

"Tell me about her," she says. "What did she look like?"

I sigh. We walk back to the window and sit at our usual table. I look into Vani's vacuous eyes.

"She was beautiful," I say. "Very curvy. Always thought she needed to lose weight but she looked perfect."

I stop. Somewhere, my mind does not make sense. I see Anjali bright and vivacious, using her hips to dance. And I see Anjali thin and frail, holding onto a window frame so as not to fall.

"Are you okay, Mol?"

"Yes. Yes."

"She was beautiful," I say. "She had light-brown eyes, golden at times. And she loved makeup. Anjali looked stunning. 'Giorgio Armani foundation, Lancôme liner,' she would say."

"Mol?"

I lose my thought like a paper kite in the sky.

"Mol, why do you say *was* and not *is*?"

I start to breathe unevenly, like a tempest rocking a boat.

I look into her eyes and somehow, I am tired of pretending. Somehow, I cannot revive Anjali again. And I am scared.

"I lied to you, Vani. She is dead. But here, with you, it was so good to believe she was alive. But you are my friend. And I lied to you. And I am sorry."

I run out of the kitchen and to my room.

Tony stirs.

"You okay there?"

"Yes."

"Should I call a doctor? Do you want some meds?"

"Please don't. I just want to calm down. I promise."

For reasons I don't understand, he listens. And then I crawl into bed. And then I fall into bed. And I stare at the vacant ceiling as it mirrors my vacant soul.

Tony watches me.

"Alisha?"

"Please don't call anyone."

"She died, Alisha. And you loved her. And I am sorry."

That is the most genuine Tony has ever been. And I have no words for him.

I close my eyes tight. It is as if the darkness outside the window has hidden itself behind my eyelids. Tighter. The darkness will not go away.

"*She died, Alisha.*"

I know it is true. But I do not believe that it is true. Do I not owe it to Anjali to feel the loss of her? I fall asleep slowly and wonder if Vani is angry with me.

Today I wait, as always, for Tony to fall asleep. He is still sitting in the chair, saying nothing. Two o'clock seems far away. I wait. Eventually, I hear the flutter of a snore. I watch to make sure he is sleeping. Then I quietly walk past Tony and enter the kitchen. According to the orange clock on the far wall, it is four past two.

When I see Vani, she does not mention my apology. We sit at the table by the window. Steam rises from her plastic container but she does not eat. She stares out of the window at the darkness as if searching for answers or answering a great question.

"Once you know, once I had dog. I loved that dog. He was gray and white and so light I could pick him up and walk throughout Kerala. And one day a bus hit him. It took me a long time to know he was gone. My mind knew, no? My soul could not know. I used to fill his food twice a day and his water also. And I used to scream at him for not eating. But he was dead. For everyone who had eyes, he had died. But not for me. And then one day he came to me in dreams and said 'Vani, what you do? I am dead Vani. You know this.' And I did know. And I cried. And I let sadness come in."

I stare at her. For a long time we say nothing. She does not touch her food.

"What are you saying?"

She shakes her head from side to side.

"Nothing, Mol."

She presses a wad of paper towels into my palm.

"To open later," she says.

I put the package in my pocket.

We sit in silence, our eyes staring into the darkness as if there is something to find there. Nothing comes.

As Vani rises to get some water, I say it.

"She died of leukemia seventy-nine days ago. Same night I tried to kill myself."

I feel emptier than I ever have. And then something starts to seep into me. Do we call this reality or grief or love? All the same, no?

I close my eyes.

"Is that why you tried to kill yourself, Mol?"

"No. Bad timing."

I laugh a little and feel very guilty. I tried so hard to sever life with a slicing of my wrists while Anjali fought to live until she flatlined and died. Where is the justice in that?

Vani covers her uneaten dinner.

"I go now. Next time, I hope you tell me they are letting you go home."

"I have no home."

"We carry home within us, Mol. Like we do all that we love. And for these things we carry, we must be better than we think we can be."

"They won't let me go home until I feel. Until I cry. And I can't."

She gently touches my head before leaving. A blessing I guess.

I close my eyes. I do not know if it is the meds or this night or Vani or me. But this night I remember more than my girl's curves. I remember her diminishing before me. And every time I was scared, she was not.

"There is no room for fear," she would say.

Through transfusions and chemo and all of it, her leukemia grew stronger and somehow, so did she. And then one day, she couldn't grow anymore, like a tree with knotted roots. And she stopped fighting whatever wanted to take her. And then she died. She died. She died in a hospital as I slit my wrists halfway across New York City.

Let me make one thing clear. I did not try to kill myself because she died. I tried to kill myself because I was alive and it did not feel natural to breathe. I live in a world where I know there is good and bad. It is not enough for me to want to belong to it. But then in a pouring rain I met Anjali who made me feel that there was also love in this vastness. And I am guilty because even then, it was not enough for me to want to live. Somehow the shadows that play inside my mind consume me. And I am tired.

I still see her. I remember her body and how it shrank from curves and voluptuousness to taut skin and protruding bones. And even if I do not close my eyes, I can see her as if she is floating in front of me. The last words I heard her say were whispered on the phone the night before. I had gone back from the hospital to our home and she called me. We spoke for three minutes and forty-eight seconds at the end of which she said, "Baby, there is no room for fear. I will die, you will live and you know what? You will love again."

But all love is not the same. She could run a finger across my lips and take my anger from me. She could kiss the corner of my eye and swallow a tear until no more tears would come. She could rub my temples with her palms and make sleep take me. I do not believe anyone understands these rituals. I do not believe anyone understood our love.

When all is quiet and I am sure there is no one who will enter the kitchen, I unfold Vani's paper napkins. Here are two lychees side by side, attached by a stem, the skin course and maroon and bursting with fruit. I kneel on the floor and slowly peel back the rugged skin on one. I close my eyes and breathe and I can feel her fingers close to my face, urging me to use smell and touch and taste.

"This is you," I say and my throat catches.

"This is you," I say again, "full of scents and ripe with life even though they tell me you are dead."

"And this," I whisper as I hold the unpeeled fruit, looking even more maroon in contrast to the white pulp in my hand, "this is me. Rugged and coarse and unfeeling, even as I live."

I squeeze the lychees in my palm until the juice runs onto the floor. I hold them close to my chest. Nothing brings me peace. Nothing ever will. No one understood our love.

I lick lychee juice off the floor. I smell and taste and then smear the juice on the tiles. Tears spill with no kisses to land upon my eyes. I finally feel the loss of her. And the saltiness of my loss mixes with the sweetness of lychee juice. And nothing will ever be the same.

"Anjali!" I scream.

Can she hear me?

"Anjali!"

As I rock myself back and forth, she comes to me. She is here. Can't you smell the lychee juice on her fingertips?

"I am so scared without you," I say.

Somewhere in the night, before they come to lift me off the floor and sedate me with drugs I cannot pronounce, I hear her whisper.

"There is no room for fear."

But there is, my beloved, room for grief. There is room enough in the void that is me for me to understand words like *never* as in "I will never find your fragrance in the wind again" or "I will never hold you close to me when the world is too big and I am too small."

Life without you is so full of all the wrong things.
"There is no room for fear."
And yet fear consumes me.
I have never been afraid to die, my love.
But I am terrified to live.

DIVYA SOOD is the author of three novels, the latest being Find Someone to Love (Riverdale Avenue Books, 2019). She studied Creative Writing and English at Rutgers University. While at Rutgers, she was awarded the NJ Chapter of Arts and Letters First Prize for Fiction, the Edna N. Herzberg First Prize for Fiction, and the Edith Hamilton First Prize for Fiction. She pursued graduate work and earned a Master of Arts in English from New York University (NYU). She has attended the Breadloaf Writers Conference. She currently teaches at Gotham Writers Workshop in New York City, NY and is an adjunct professor of Creative Writing at Southern New Hampshire University (SNHU).

CPSIA information can be obtained
at www.ICGtesting.com
Printed in the USA
FFHW020050161219
56864031-62518FF